Denson
6 aa

# The Wrong Boy

Anna-Louise Weatherley is the former editor and acting editor of *J-17* and *Smash Hits* respectively. An award winning journalist, she has written for magazines including *Grazia*, *Arena*, *New Woman*, *Company* and *More* for over a decade. Although having recently swapped inner city London life for the relative quiet of the suburbs, she still boasts an encyclopedic knowledge of London's vintage clothing stores, which she regularly scours for pieces to add to her dress, bikini and shoe obsession. *The Wrong Boy* is her second novel.

ANNA-LOUISE WEATHERLEY

# The Wrong Boy

Piccadilly Press • London

*For Suse and Maya, my Portobello pals.*

*I'd like to thank everyone at Piccadilly Press, in particular
Brenda Gardner, Anne Clark and Melissa Patey for all their help
and support; all at CosmoGIRL!, especially Celia Duncan, and last, but
never least, Alan and Louie, my best boys ever. This one's for you two!*

First published in Great Britain in 2007
by Piccadilly Press Ltd,
5 Castle Road, London NW1 8PR
www.piccadillypress.co.uk

Text copyright © Anna-Louise Weatherley, 2007

A catalogue record for this book is available from the British Library

ISBN: 978 1 85340 912 7 (trade paperback)

1 3 5 7 9 10 8 6 4 2

Printed in the UK by CPI Bookmarque, Croydon, CR0 4TD
Typeset by Textype, Cambridge, based on a design by Louise Millar
Cover design by Sue Hellard and Simon Davis
Set in StempelGaramond and Carumba

The expression CosmoGIRL! is the registered trademark of the
National Magazine Company Ltd and the Hearst Corporation

'Where Love Lives', written by Lars Kronlund.
Published by BMG Music Publishing Ltd. Used by permission.
All rights reserved. Performed by Alison Limerick.

F
WEA

'So you're longing for the
warmth of somebody,
You've got nothing in this
world to lose.
Let me take you down where
love lives,
Come away, come on out of
your blues.'

**'Where Love Lives'**
**Alison Limerick**

# Chapter 1

I put the last of the boxes on the floor, let out a long sigh and sat down on top of it. I looked over at Mums, standing by the curtainless window, its peeling paintwork showing the rotting wood underneath. She seemed to be staring out at something of great interest. I let out another sigh, mainly to let her know I was there. She didn't turn round but carried on absent-mindedly tearing little strips off the newspaper which had been used to wrap my alarm clock.

'Trust us to move on such a freakishly hot day,' I said, wiping the perspiration from my forehead with the back of my hand. The intensity of the heat gave the unfamiliar room a faintly familiar smell, musky like wood smoke, as if the sun was burning through the bare floorboards.

It wouldn't be such a bad thing if this house did go up in flames, I thought to myself, feeling instantly guilty. I looked down at my flip-flop clad feet. They had begun to throb from all the lifting and carrying I had done, and I noticed the pink pearl nail varnish on my toenails had started to chip and peel away, just like the shoddy paintwork in the room.

'Well, look at it this way: at least you'll be able to perfect your tan in the garden,' Mums said, without turning away from the window. 'I know it's not much but it's all ours, you know.'

'Yippee!' I muttered sarcastically. I was careful not to let her hear me, though, because I sensed that underneath her fake cheerfulness she felt as miserable as I did.

'Anyway,' she said, quickly changing the subject and finally turning away from the window, 'what do you think of your new room, then? A lick of paint and some decent lighting should see it looking OK, don't you think?'

'I suppose it'll do,' I said as cheerily as I could muster. This was the first time I had seen my new bedroom. I cast my eyes over the dusty floorboards, searching for a redeeming feature. A lone light bulb hung solemnly in the middle of the ceiling and a spiteful-looking crack ran the length of one dishwater grey wall.

'I know it's not ideal,' Mums said quietly, following my gaze, 'but I'm afraid it will have to do . . . for now at least.'

I nodded. Now was not the time for arguments.

'Let's try and think of it as a holiday,' she added brightly, that awful fake grin on her face making her look like a waxwork dummy. 'Something temporary until . . . well, until things sort themselves out.'

I scanned the room again, hoping my imagination might spring into life, paint it a vibrant colour and fill it with beautiful things, but I could not take my eyes off that horrible crack in the wall.

'I thought, as the weather is so lovely, we might start by getting the garden in order,' Mums continued. 'Maybe even make a nice lunch to eat on the patio – once we find it under the foliage, that is.'

'You? *Cook* lunch?' I tried not to look shocked. Mums's idea of cooking amounted to opening a can of beans, pouring them in a bowl and pressing the start button on a microwave. Fabienne, one of our house-keepers, had always been the chief cook in our house. Besides, Mums was always too busy with her charity lunches, shopping expeditions or ladies' golfing tourna-ments to be stuck in a kitchen all day.

'Well, I was thinking more *prepare*,' she said.

I laughed. I thought I saw a flicker of a smile creep across her lips too. It made me feel momentarily happy.

'I suppose it's do-able,' I responded, adding, 'clearing the garden, I mean, not you cooking – sorry, *preparing* lunch.

'That's the spirit, darling,' she said, her enthusiasm returning. 'We'll have this place looking divine in no time. Anyway, where would you like these?' She held up my lava lamp – a much-loved present from Tave for my fifteenth birthday (we were going through our psychedelic hippie phase at the time) – like a trophy in one hand and my framed print of Salvador Dali's infamous 'Swans and Elephants' – a gift from Dad – in the other. My parents had tons of art scattered all over our house, not surprising as Dad was an art and antiques dealer.

I shrugged, resignedly. 'I think it's going to take a bit more than a Dali to sort *this* room out.'

Mums's grin began to fade. It was her turn to sigh this time. 'This is not easy for *any* of us you know, Gracie,' she said, wrinkling her turned-up nose. 'We have to make the best of it . . . '

' . . . and pull together as a family,' I said, finishing her sentence for her. I hadn't meant it to sound so sarcastic. (Note to self: must remember that sarcasm is the lowest form of wit.) Poor Mums, I thought. None of this could be easy for her either. My mother, the salon queen, who always has her hair styled twice a week; Mums, who is regularly buffed, tweezered, scoured, scrubbed and polished to within an inch of her life, thanks to some expensive new fad she's been talked into trying. I sighed yet again and wondered how she would be able to afford to feed her beauty addiction now. I felt ashamed of myself for taking it out on her. None of this was her doing. She was right. We needed to pull together.

Cal burst into the room, breaking the heavy silence between us.

'It's the hottest August day recorded in British history – *ever!*' he panted excitedly, as if he had discovered this fact himself. 'An old person has died through heat exhaustion and everything! I saw it on the news.'

'That's terrible, Cal,' I said, seriously.

'Isn't it?' he replied, and I couldn't help but smile at how grown up he sounded. Cal was only just twelve but sometimes he came out with things that made him sound much older. I sometimes referred to him as 'Little Lord Fauntleroy', which he hated of course, and in turn he would call me 'Grace-less'. I adored him.

'*You'll* help with the garden, won't you, Tigs?' Mums said, turning to Cal (Tigs was Mums's nickname for Cal, on account of him being a 'very bouncy' baby), 'I'm sure I saw the removal men bring the lawn mower. You go down,' she added, 'and leave Grouch-o-Marx here to unpack her make-up. It should only take her . . . ohh, about three weeks!'

Cal started to laugh.

'Oh ha ha, *très* amusing,' I scoffed. Secretly, though, I was glad she was poking fun at me – it was as if she was her old self again.

Cal skipped out of the room. 'See you in three weeks, Grace-less,' he called out gleefully. Despite everything, Cal seemed annoyingly happy, as if he were actually pleased to be here, like this was all just one big adventure to him. I wished I could share his enthusiasm. Once he had left the room, Mums's face reverted to being serious.

'You didn't open the letter, then,' she said, a little sadly, looking at the small white envelope I had carefully placed on an old cabinet next to my bed.

'No,' I replied, quietly.

She sighed yet again. I could tell it was going to be a day for sighing. 'I wish you would, Gracie. Dad made me promise . . . '

I stared down at my feet and began to shuffle from side to side a little. (Note to self: must do express pedicure as a matter of extreme urgency.)

'Anyway,' Mums said, wisely deciding not to push the point, 'I know this place is not exactly Embers, but it's really rather an interesting area once you get to know it, or so I'm told. And Portobello Market is just down the road. You'll be able to indulge your passion for vintage clothing, darling.'

Mums certainly knew how to push my buttons. She was well aware of my love of dressing up and all things theatrical. As a child, I constantly raided her vast wardrobe, and I would strut around Embers – our old house – in one or other of her glamorous cocktail dresses, pretending to be a famous old-time Hollywood actress like Ava Gardner or Greta Garbo, and standing in front of the mirror practising my Oscar acceptance speeches (note the plural; I planned to win at least five).

'Anyway,' she continued, 'it'll be fun starting a new school and making new friends. Meeting new people is always exciting.' She sounded like she was trying to convince herself as much as me.

New friends, I thought. I didn't want new friends. I had liked the ones I had, thanks all the same. But I said nothing. I simply nodded and attempted a smile.

'Good girl,' she said. 'Things will come right, mark my words. You might even enjoy it here!' Now she really was pushing it. 'I'll be in the garden with Cal. Perhaps you'll come and help once you've finished here?'

I nodded again. I couldn't bring myself to speak. I was too frightened of what might come out of my mouth.

'And Gracie,' she added, giving me her best pleading face, 'promise me you'll read the letter?'

I didn't want to promise but I said 'OK, Mums,' just to get her to leave.

I waited until she had closed the door behind her before putting to one side the few boxes that contained what was left of the sixteen years of my life so far, and walked over towards the window. I was intrigued to see what had held her attention for so long. I looked out on to the garden. Overgrown grass and dandelions covered the postage stamp-sized area. Broken stones made a small path through the middle and, somewhere beneath the weeds, a tiny patio was just visible. Apart from a lone apple tree at the back, there was nothing, not a shrub or a rosebush in sight.

I sighed for the gazillionth time that day. Mums had told me that the new house (actually rather an old house, built in the late 1800s) had been vacant for some time and that one of Dad's more sympathetic 'associates' had kindly offered to let us rent it at a 'ridiculously reduced' price. It was easy to see why. A large and ugly railway track ran right behind our garden wall. Trains would be passing through at all hours of the day and night, keeping me awake. Great.

I saw that the tall brick wall on the far side of the railway tracks was completely covered in colourful graffiti and I squinted in an attempt to make sense of the mass of scribbles. One piece stood out above the others. It was a picture of a bird with the word 'DOVE' written in bright blue, grey and white block-style letters above it.

Behind the brick wall, a dirty brown tower block glared back at me, its imposing height threatening to block out the sun. Laundry hung lifelessly from tiny balconies cluttered with bicycles and acid-bright plastic kids' toys; England flags hung in windows instead of curtains. I counted a couple of boarded-up windows and doors – one black with fire damage. It was the most depressing view I had ever seen in my life, yet I found myself strangely mesmerised by it, just as I think Mums had been earlier.

A train abruptly sounded its horn, making me jump as it passed the end of our garden. Another quickly followed it in the opposite direction.

'Welcome to your new home Grace Foster-Bryce,' I said to myself miserably.

Despite being exhausted from the day's lifting, carrying, sorting and grass cutting, that night I could not sleep. I looked at my phone: 23.16.

I wondered if Tave would still be up and, even if she was, would she reply to me if I texted her? Although we had not exactly fallen out, I had noticed that she'd been more distant with me recently, especially since I'd announced we were moving away.

*Hiya, wot u up 2? G x*

I was pleased when she texted me straight back.

*Hi, howz the nu house? Have u settled in yet? Saw BSJ at Nubis 2day. Sigh. T x*

Nubis was a sushi bar in Richmond upon Thames, the hangout *du jour* that played cool music and served the most exquisite sashimi and tempura, and BSJ (Bradley Stanley-Jones) was Tave's latest love interest. I pictured my friends there having fun and felt utterly crushed. It wasn't as if I expected them to stay in and mope about my absence, but I couldn't help feeling that they had all just moved on so quickly, so effortlessly.

Nothing had changed for them and *everything* had changed for me.

*Keep me updated with BSJ stuff. Maybe u and Legs will come down 2 C me soon? G x*

She didn't respond.

Rejected, I closed my eyes and tried to think about nothing in particular, but my brain had other ideas and, even though I made a concerted effort to sway my thoughts in the direction of something – *anything* – else, I started to think about Dad and what he might be doing right now. I wondered if he was sleeping, or lying in a cold bed unable to close his eyes for thinking about me. Was he happily chatting with the other criminals, or playing chess like they always seem to do in the TV shows? I wondered who he might be sharing a cell with (I had never asked and Mums had never said). I hoped it was someone he could talk to about art, travel and the theatre (our shared passion), but I was worried it was more likely to be someone with a name like Gripper, a homicidal maniac with gold teeth and homemade tattoos.

I closed my eyes tightly and began reciting my times tables, something I used to do as a child to help me to drop off to sleep. 'Four fours are sixteen, five fours are twenty, six fours are twenty-four, seven fours are twenty-eight, eight fours are thirty-two, nine fours are . . . ' and eventually I fell asleep to the clack-clack sound of passing trains and sirens wailing in the distance.

# Chapter 2

**M**y life during the last twelve months has been as surreal and freaky as a Dali painting. Let me explain.

On a chilly October evening last year Mums dropped a huge bombshell on us.

'Your father has been arrested. Suspicion of fraud or something ludicrous,' she'd snorted dismissively. 'Our solicitor is dealing with it, so I don't want you or Cal to be alarmed.'

Alarmed? How was *that* for an understatement? Although Mums was trying to be calm, she was manically twisting a piece of her hair between her fingers and she only ever does that under extreme pressure.

'I'm sure it's all a big mistake,' she'd added, waving her free hand frantically.

But here's a thing: it turned out that it wasn't a big mistake at all. Dad, *my* dad, had been selling fake works of art! Apparently, he was part of some international swindle where fake classical paintings were commissioned and then sold on to unsuspecting wealthy clients and art galleries across the world for humongous sums of money, which, incidentally, had never been declared to the taxman.

Overnight, our idyllic life was turned upside down.

Oxshott Village, the picturesque, commuter belt suburb of Surrey where we lived, was not the kind of place where any such scandal went unnoticed, particularly since we were considered upstanding members of its small but wealthy community. Everybody knew the Foster-Bryces. We lived at Embers, one of the most impressive houses in the village, which sat in three acres of land, complete with outdoor swimming pool and tennis court.

Embers' gardens, or grounds as Mums liked to call them, were huge and filled with herbaceous borders, wisteria and flowering cherry, crab apple and magnolia trees. Wild roses grew along the two arbours on either side of the vast decked patio where Mums like to hold gatherings for all our wealthy friends and neighbours, and Dad liked to smoke a cigar and drink homemade sloe gin that our housekeepers, Max and Fabienne, made from sloes picked from the blackthorn bushes.

Summer was my favourite season. It meant I could spend as much time as possible lounging around the swimming pool with Tave and Legs, sipping cream soda and trying to get a decent tan, which is no mean feat when you're naturally a lighter shade of pale. It took real dedication.

I attended Oakwood College for Young Ladies, a private school with an exemplary record that claimed to 'make ladies' out of all its pupils. Dad often joked that, 'at five thousand pounds a term, I want her to come away with the *title* of Lady!' which never failed to amuse guests at the lavish parties my parents threw. Swot or not (and admittedly I was probably more the former), I loved school. Oakwood was my life. My *social* life. Each year the school held two special events: the Christmas party and, by far my favourite, a Grand Summer Ball. The Summer Ball was held in conjunction with St Benedict's Boys college and all us Oakies (as we called ourselves) would spend months preparing our outfits for what we considered the event of the year in the hope of bagging ourselves a rich St Ben's boy – ideally one with a whopping great trust fund.

Tave and I loved the Summer Ball and all the gossip it generated. My best friend Tave (Octavia Petronella Wyatt) is an aristocratic blonde with aqua blue eyes and a perfect pout that people wrongly assume she's acquired through collagen injections. I, on the other hand, have lack-lustre auburn hair that hangs limply to my shoulders, a snub nose (courtesy of Mums) and freckles that always appear much more prominent during the summer months. Tave is all va-va-voom curves and accentuated cleavage, while I'm on the gangly side of tall – straight up and down, with flat tyres. Thank the Lord for chicken-fillet bras, I used to say to Tave.

When I wasn't at school, I spent most of my time hanging out with Tave and sometimes with Legs (Allegra Cleopatra Bahiti). When it came to wealth, Legs' parents were in a league of their own. Related to Egyptian royalty (their surname means fortune in Arabic), they had outdoor *and* indoor swimming pools, a mini gym annexe in their grounds and seven full-time staff. I wasn't sure how much money we, the Foster-Bryces, had, or whether the money we did have had been earned or inherited or a bit of both. All I knew was that I had never wanted for anything in my entire life. Looking back, I had no idea just how privileged I was. I never thought of myself as particularly posh or wealthy. In my world it was normal to own a horse, a wardrobe filled with expensive designer clothes and a five hundred pound monthly allowance to spend on anything you liked. My worries amounted to what to wear on a Saturday night and, more importantly, what boys might be out and about. Tough decisions, huh?

Upon sentencing Dad six months later, the judge had said that 'it was regrettable that such a fine member of the community had let greed cloud his otherwise impeccable judgement' and that 'despite his previously unblemished character,' he had no alternative but to grant him a custodial sentence befitting his crimes. He sent him down for four years with a recommendation that he serve at least eighteen months. Apparently, this was considered a 'successful' outcome but for whom I am not sure.

In the weeks that followed, I watched helplessly as our perfect life gradually unravelled, bit by bit. Mums spent most of the time chain-smoking her way through long and fraught telephone conversations and crying a lot. She didn't venture out too much either. I think she was ashamed as much as anything. 'Her husband's in jail, don't you know. Terrible business,' she would hear the prittle-prattlers mutter. It nearly destroyed her.

Then, halfway through the summer holidays, just as I had thought things could not get any worse, Mums had broken yet more bad news to us – only this time she couldn't manage to hide her anguish. Cal and I stood solemnly as we watched black tears roll down Mums's cheeks.

'Listen, darlings,' she said, dabbing her eyes with a tissue and smudging her mascara, 'we're going to have to move from Embers.' She was choking on her words as she spoke. I handed her another tissue. 'Unfortunately, we have been declared bankrupt.'

'Bankrupt,' I repeated nervously.

'Yes,' she snapped, irritated. 'We will have to sell Embers, and most of its contents, plus the house in Florence, the cars, and the antiques shop to pay for your father's legal costs and to reimburse the taxman. Not to mention compensate some of the *supposed* "victims",' she added bitterly, 'as if they need the money!'

So there it was. The creditors were moving in and we were moving out. We would have to leave our beautiful home, our schools and our friends – what was left of them. But worse than all of that, we were going to be *poor*. To me, the concept of being poor amounted to buying only one designer dress instead of two; I had no idea what it really meant. But I would soon find out.

# Chapter 3

I could see the top of the tower block as we walked along Goldborne Road. Its ominous height over-shadowed the other smaller blocks like a bully in a playground.

'I suppose it could be worse,' I said to Cal, looking up in the tower's direction. 'We could live *there*.'

'That's Hamlet Tower,' Cal said casually, as if he'd lived in this area for years and not just two weeks. 'It's mainly social housing, although I think some apartments might now be privately owned. Designed and built by quite a famous architect in the early Seventies.'

'How do you know all this, Little Lord Fauntleroy?' I asked, impressed by his local knowledge.

'I've been researching the area on the internet. And don't call me *that*,' he said, giving me a little shove and causing me to swerve, narrowly avoiding some dog mess on the pavement.

It was eight-fifteen on a Monday morning and Goldborne Road was just starting to wake up. Shopkeepers were beginning to open their premises and people were arranging chairs and tables outside the cafés and restaurants that lined the road. The September breeze blew Cal's blond hair back and I pulled my cardigan over my shoulders. The summer holidays were over, and suddenly I couldn't go out in just a vest-top or T-shirt, which made me feel a little miserable. Winter was coming and with it dark nights and cold, grey days. Worse, I faced the daunting prospect of starting a new school. And this was not just another school year, as Mums kept reminding me – I would be taking my AS-levels next summer. Years of hard (and expensive) study would finally start to pay off, getting me the grades I needed to continue into the Upper Sixth and then on to university – at least, that was the theory. Only I wouldn't be doing any of it in the comfort and familiar surroundings of my beloved Oakwood with my beloved friends. No, instead I would be alone in some run-down inner-city comprehensive with a reputation worthy of an appearance on *Crimewatch*.

A pungent waft of fish filled my nose as we walked past the fishmonger's. Inside, harried-looking men in their bloodstained aprons were hacking through giant hunks of tuna.

'Hey,' one of them called out to us as he held a fish up in our direction, 'nice *plaice* we got here!' The men inside the shop groaned with laughter. A large, grey fish lay on a metal slab, the morning sun catching the rainbow colours of its skin. The poor thing looked quite beautiful. Open-mouthed, it looked surprised, as if it had been happily going about its fishy business in a lake or river or wherever, and then . . . gotcha! I looked at the creature's dead eyes and felt an infinite sympathy. Like me, he hadn't seen his fate coming. (Note to self: must remember never to eat fish again.)

'You can always tell the quality of a fishmonger's by its smell,' Cal said as we walked on. I held my nose. 'If it has the aroma of the sea that means it's a good one, but if it just stinks of fish, that means it's not so good.'

'What *are* you talking about?' I said through pinched nose.

'It's true!' Cal protested.

'How do you *know* these things?!' I laughed, letting go of my nose once I was convinced it was safe to do so. 'Don't tell me you've been researching local fishmonger's as well!'

'I don't know how I know,' Cal shrugged. 'I just do.'

I shook my head incredulously and thought how much Cal was like Dad – a fount of obscure information.

'So are you looking forward to starting your new school then?' I asked. I couldn't help worrying what the local kids would make of my eccentric little brother.

'I suppose.' Cal shrugged his shoulders. I looked at him, unconvinced. 'It's a pity they don't have a rowing team though.'

From the outside, Kinsmead Comprehensive School looked like the prison my dad now calls home. Or at least, it was how I imagined the prison – I had never visited Dad at Altringham because my parents had agreed that it was best for me and Cal not to. Dad was adamant he did not want his children exposed to such an environment. Mums said he would rather we wrote to him, talked to him through letters. I had protested at first.

'But it'll be literally *years* until we see him again!' I shrieked, annoyed that they had come to this decision without even asking what Cal and I might want to do.

'It's not that he doesn't *want* to see you, Gracie,' Mums had argued. 'He just wants to protect you. Try to think of it as a long business trip. The solicitor reckons that he'll be out on good behaviour in less than eight months. It won't be long now and you can write every day if you like.'

But I knew a letter would simply not cut it. I didn't want Dad to hide behind the safety of written words and not have to look me in the eye. I wanted explanations as to how we had ended up in this mess and I wanted him to tell me to my face! Whenever I had broached the subject with Mums, she would sigh a little and say 'he did it for us, Gracie. For you and me and Cal,' and that's as much as I would get. I resented her for not being more honest with me. It irked me that she didn't think me mature enough to be able to handle the truth.

'He is still your father, whatever he's done,' she would say as she watched me rip up another unopened letter. It irritated me how easily Mums had forgiven Dad for everything that had happened. She'd even fallen out with her own mother, my Grandma Violet, about the situation and they hadn't spoken for months. 'I made vows, Gracie,' she said unwaveringly, 'for richer *or* for poorer.'

I pushed through the cold, slate-grey bars of the school gate, said goodbye to Cal and made my way through the unfamiliar corridors. I was looking for classroom 3B, only I kept losing my bearings and soon ended up back where I had started. People on their way to lessons rushed past me as if I was invisible. I was too nervous to ask anyone for directions. Luckily, I overheard a couple of girls mention something about an English lesson in 3B and so I followed them and hoped for the best.

'OK, people, settle down,' the grey-haired man said. I presumed he must be the teacher although I couldn't be sure; he was very scruffy, with an open-necked shirt that was the sort of colour shirts go when your housekeeper accidentally leaves a black sock in with the white washing. It had a button missing, and tufts of horrible thick, black hair poked out of the top of his collar. His trousers, slightly creased, looked a little short for his legs too. He could very well have been the caretaker.

'Well, guys, welcome back. It's great to see some of you have decided to stay with us for another year. Good choice, folks, good choice. I trust you all enjoyed the holidays. I certainly did because I got to be away from you lot! Ha! The wife and I spent two lovely weeks sunning ourselves on the Amalfi Coast, sipping *limoncello* and enjoying the splendid view from our balcony.' He rubbed his hands together enthusiastically before continuing. 'I'm sure you've all been extremely busy swotting up on your schoolwork over the summer hols, eh?' He raised an eyebrow. 'I don't need to tell you that this year is a vital year for you guys, lots of hard work I'm afraid, people, lots of hard work.'

There was some groaning as people began to chatter.

'Okey-cokey,' he said, clapping his hands together suddenly, 'Oh, before I forget, we have a new face to welcome. Grace Foster-Rice, is it?' he said, squinting around the room.

'Bryce,' I said, quietly, 'Foster-Bryce.' I felt myself flush crimson as the entire room turned round to look at me.

'Bryce, right, yes, there you are. Huge apols, Brycie. I'm Mr Dickins. No relation to the great man himself, regrettably, but head of the English and drama departments nonetheless, so welcome to my English literature A-level class and welcome to Kinsmead Comprehensive. I hope you'll be very happy here. Just as I am,' he said, placing his hand on his heart and dramatically fluttering his eyes. I think he was being sarcastic. 'I see you didn't do so bad in your GCSE English, Brycie. Great. I'll be looking for big things from you then this year.'

It felt like a thousand pair of eyes were boring holes into me, and I thought I heard someone laughing. I wasn't sure how to respond so I nodded. 'Yes sir. Of course.'

More sniggers.

He clasped his hands together again. 'Okey-cokey, jiggery-pokey. Let's kick off as we mean to go on. William Blake. Anyone heard of him?'

There were a few murmurs of acknowledgement.

'Best you get yourselves familiar with this name, pronto,' said Mr Dickins, pacing the room and throwing what looked like exercise books at people. I took the opportunity to have a clandestine look around me. There was a mixture of girls and boys huddled together in small groups. Some were sitting up on the desks; others were casually leaning back on their chairs. As I had attended same sex schools all my life, it was a novelty to see boys in a classroom with girls, not to mention a little exciting. Maybe there would be some half-decent boy for me to look at, to help make this whole experience a little more bearable. I scanned the room but wasn't too impressed. Most of the boys looked a bit sneery and unfriendly. But it was early days. I still had the whole school to explore. The girls all looked rather alike, in a strange way. Most seemed to wear their hair harshly scraped back from their faces in low ponytails or in tight cornrows that exposed their scalps. They dressed in a sort of anti-uniform of jeans and sports tops or combat pants and tight T-shirts with slogans. One particular brunette girl's read *Stop staring at my boobs!* which seemed to have the opposite effect. Perhaps that was the point. I couldn't believe that she was allowed to attend school dressed like that. At Oakwood you would be sent home to change immediately.

'Yeah?' the girl spat, catching me looking. 'Can I help you?' She narrowed her dark, kohl-rimmed eyes as she glared at me. I noticed that her lip liner was much darker than her lipstick, giving her face an almost clown-like appearance.

Nervous, I found myself inappropriately wanting to laugh. 'Sorry, I, er . . . I was just admiring your T-shirt actually,' I spluttered shakily.

'Well, *actually,* don't, all right?' she snapped, before turning back to her friends.

'Yah, I was just admiring your T-shirt *actually, jolly smashing, what!*' I heard them mimic me. I shifted anxiously in my seat. I wondered what my friends at Oakwood were doing right at that moment. They were probably in the common room (which wasn't in the least bit common), drinking Earl Grey tea and discussing the weekend's antics. We had been looking forward to starting Sixth Form together. It was all so unfair.

'So, Blake. Blakey, good ol' Bill Blakey,' Mr Dickins said. He really was quite an unusual teacher. 'Anyone know much about him?'

The room was suddenly silent but for the loud clacking sound of someone chewing gum. 'Anybody?'

'He's a poet, sir,' a small blond-haired girl said.

'Spot on, Samuels, spot on.' Mr Dickins seemed to have a habit of saying everything twice. 'He was in fact the Sloop P or Raze-R of his day.'

Now I am no rap aficionado or anything – I prefer pop or film soundtracks, even a bit of classical if I'm totally honest – but I'd read somewhere that Sloop P and Raze-R were these legendary underground hip-hop artists from LA. I was seriously impressed that a teacher would know about them.

'Anyone else . . . ?'

I slowly raised my hand.

'Ah, good. Brycie. Yes . . . well . . . ?'

'He was a poet, sir . . . '

'Durrr,' said someone behind me, 'we gathered that.'

' . . . and a painter and engraver. He illustrated all his own books . . . '

'Indeed he did, Brycie . . . '

I heard the sound of low whispers from behind me.

'Anyone familiar with any of his poetry, or is that really asking *far* too much?' Mr Dickins scanned the room hopefully.

'I know!' a boy called out from the back. He was wearing a sports T-shirt and had a heavy gold chain around his neck. He was balancing the back of his chair against the classroom wall. 'He wrote about London or something,' he said. He pronounced 'something' as 'sumfink.'

'Well, Pipkin, miracles really *do* happen,' Mr Dickins said. 'Yes, dear Mr Blake *did* indeed write a poem entitled 'London'. I don't suppose you could actually *recite* any of it for us at all?' He looked at 'Pipkin' expectantly.

Pipkin shrugged. 'Only know the title, sir.'

We had touched on a little of Blake's work last year at Oakwood. I was given an assignment to write about one of his poems and had chosen 'The Sick Rose'. I had decided that it was about 'an all-consuming passionate desire that went unreciprocated' and that the poet was 'expressing his vulnerability and pain at being in love with someone who didn't love him back'. It was quite appropriate at the time as I had a massive crush on Hugo Sanderson (along with half of Oakwood) and he'd never even so much as looked at me, not once. Ever. Still, I got a B+ for it.

'O Rose, *thou art sick!*
*The invisible worm*

*That flies in the night,*
*In the howling storm,*
*Has found out thy bed*
*Of crimson joy:*
*And his dark secret love*
*Does thy life destroy.'*

As my mind drifted towards thoughts of Hugo Sanderson, I absent-mindedly began to recite the poem softly to myself, unaware that the girl sitting at the next desk could hear me. Instinctively I clasped my hand over my mouth. The girl and, by the end, a few others too, erupted into hysterical laughter.

'*Get her!*' she screamed between her hysterics. 'Oh rose thou art sick,' she gasped dramatically. My instinct told me to run out of the classroom, but instead I just sat there like a lump, head bowed, my ears burning with embarrassment.

'Settle down!' Mr Dickins said, more loudly this time and with much more force.

It was more than a relief when the bell for break finally rang and I could escape the sniggers and stares of my classmates.

I read the graffiti as I sat alone and miserable on the playground bench: *KAZ LOVES MARSHY, LINA DAVIES IS A SLUT, LIPGLOSSROCKERS LIVIN' LARGE.* I felt like adding *GRACE FOSTER-BRYCE IS A COMPLETE PRAT,* but I didn't have a pen handy and besides, knowing my luck, I would only get caught. I rifled around my bag in search of my mobile – but who could I call? Tave and Legs would never understand what Kinsmead was like, and anyway I felt too ashamed to tell them. I couldn't ring Mums because she would only worry. I'd never felt so lonely in my life.

# chapter 4

A girl came over and plonked herself down next to me on the bench, breaking into my thoughts. She was on the small side with short brown hair and her round glasses, perched on the end of her nose, gave her face an almost mole-like but friendly appearance.

'Hi, I'm Jessica. Jessica Beaks,' she said, turning towards me. 'You're the new girl, right?'

I nodded.

'Thought you could use some company,' she said, smiling.

'Thanks,' I said, relieved to hear that her voice matched her friendly face. 'I was beginning to feel like a bit of an outcast.'

'Honey,' she said in a fake American accent, 'you might as well be a leper as far as this place is concerned.'

She crossed her legs and put her bag on the ground, hooking her foot inside the handles. I wasn't sure if she was trying to be helpful or not.

'Why's that?' I asked, although I didn't really want to know the answer.

'No one likes a posho round here, I'm afraid.' She sucked her breath in and made a little tutting noise.

'I never realised being posh was such a terrible thing,'

I said, miserably. 'Besides, I didn't realise I was *that* posh.'

'Oh come on,' she laughed incredulously, 'double-barrelled surname, over-pronunciation of your vowels, and a perfect recitation of Blake – you *have* to be posh.' She laughed again. 'Best you take the posh test though, just to be on the safe side.'

'The posh test?' I looked at her blankly.

'OK,' she said, smoothing her hands down the sides of her tights, then pretending to hold a clipboard. 'Do you ever end your sentences with the words *"liiike"*, *"innit"*, *"nahwotImsaying"*, or a combination of any of the aforementioned, regardless of whether you're asking a question or not?'

I searched Jessica's face for some kind of clue as to whether she was being serious.

'No. At least, I don't think so,' I replied. She made an imaginary tick on her imaginary clipboard.

'Do you live on a council estate, have you ever shoplifted and have any of your family ever been awarded an ASBO?' She made it sound like a sought-after prize.

'Er, no, no and well . . . no, not exactly an ASBO but . . . '

'Then I'm afraid to break the news to you. Round here, Ms Foster-Bryce, you are classed as posh,' she said, shaking her head as if she were a doctor giving me some bad news.

'You remembered my name,' I said, a little pleased.

'It's not a name you forget really, is it?' she replied, her head cocked to one side. 'Especially in this dump.'

I shrugged. 'I suppose not.'

'Anyway, Grace Foster-Bryce,' she said brightly, '*I'm* glad you're here.'

'You are?' I said, surprised.

'Yup indeedy, as Mr Dickins would say. I've been the posh bird of this school for long enough! Now that you're here, I'm the not-as-posh-as-you-bird, which is great!' She looked at me and then started to laugh.

I stared at her, bemused. Why couldn't I tell if anyone in this godforsaken place was joking or not?

'Just kidding,' she said, digging me lightly in the ribs. 'Lighten up. It's not so bad here once you get used to it.'

'Really?' I said, unconvinced.

'Yeah, I've only ever been beaten up twice since I got here.'

I looked at her, horrified.

'Jeez, you're *so* easy to wind up. Seriously, it really isn't as bad as everyone makes out,' she said, still smiling. 'First things first though, there are some things you need to know about Kinsmead.' She wiggled her bottom on the seat in an exaggerated attempt to get comfortable. 'Number one: Mr Dickins is as mad as a bag of frogs but he's probably one of the nicer teachers here, especially if you're into drama and all that. Some of the teachers can be quite fierce, like Mr Thorn, the business studies guy – he can be a bit scary. Rumour has it he once had a fight with a Lower Sixth pupil some years back. The boy had to have fifteen stitches in his head! Almost lost his job apparently.' Jessica must have caught the look on my face because she quickly added, 'Not sure if it's really true though; that's another thing you'll get used to – the rumours. If there's one thing Kinsmead likes, it's a good rumour. So,' she continued, looking deep in thought, 'Miss March is pretty cool. She teaches psychology. She sometimes has a smoke with the sixth-formers in the common room. Always got boyfriend troubles though. My dad heard that she was having an affair with Liam Anison's dad. Liam Anison doesn't go to this school anymore though,' she explained, 'he's in prison for arson, but he used to go out with Janice Brady. Oh God, Janice Brady.' Jessica rolled her eyes and drew breath. 'She's the one wearing the T-shirt. Did you clock her?' She didn't give me time to respond. 'I mean, how utterly pathetic. As if anyone *wants* to look at her boobs. Although I guess it is mildly preferable to looking at her face. Anyway, believe it or not, Janice got good grades last year, although rumour has it she paid someone to do most of her coursework for her.'

I swallowed. 'Right,' I said. 'I see. Thanks for the information.'

'Don't mention it,' she replied, clearly happy to be of service.

There was a moment's silence between us, which I felt compelled to fill. 'So you're not from round here originally then?' I asked.

'Canterbury, born and bred,' she said quickly and proudly. 'Dad started his own business, but it all went belly-up about five years ago and we had to move to London so that he could find work. We ended up in the daggy end of Ladbroke Grove, because it was all we could afford at the time. It's OK. You get the occasional junkie on the doorstep, but you learn to step over them. And we've only been broken into twice in five years so it could be worse.'

I laughed, but the expression on her face didn't change and I realised that this time she was being serious.

'So how come you ended up in this hell-hole? Bad day on the stock exchange for Daddy, was it?'

'It's a long story,' I said.

'And . . . ' she said, nodding encouragingly.

I had promised myself that I would not tell anyone the truth about why we had ended up here. If anyone asked, I had decided to say we had moved here on family business and leave it at that, but she caught me unawares so I did something really stupid. I told the truth.

'My dad . . . my father's in prison for fraud,' I said quietly. I was amazed at how easily the words fell from my lips, as if I were casually telling her my star sign. 'He was part of this "great" art scandal and he got caught and we had to sell our house to pay his legal fees and reimburse the taxman and Dad's "victims", so that's how we ended up in this hell-hole, as you put it.'

'Wow,' Jessica said open-mouthed. 'That certainly beats an ASBO!'

'Listen, Jessica,' I said, suddenly feeling sick with fear, 'you won't tell anyone what I've just told you, will you? It's just that I have a little brother in Year Eight and I'm worried people might pick on him if . . . '

'Hey,' she said with exaggerated graveness, holding her

hand up for me to stop, 'you are looking at the very soul of discretion.'

I wished she wouldn't make everything sound like a joke.

The bell rang, so we both got up and walked towards the Sixth Form block.

'Thanks,' I said, smiling weakly, even though I was already beginning to regret giving away my biggest secret to a complete stranger.

Cal met me at the gates after school, but he insisted on running ahead, desperate to get home in time to catch some TV documentary about World War I, so I made my way home alone through 'Sometime Place', an odd place that backed on to the canal. It was neither a park nor a garden exactly, but something in between. I guessed it was a communal space for all the hundreds of people living in the blocks and estates – for people who didn't have gardens themselves. As I made my way along the pathway by the small skate park, a couple of young boys were flipping their boards across the dips and ramps, attempting half pipes and other cool skate moves. I looked up and saw the faint trail of an aeroplane in the distance. I wished I was on it. The destination was unimportant, just so long as it would take me out of *here*. I sighed as I wondered if I would ever fit in at Kinsmead Comprehensive – a place where teachers looked like caretakers and fellow students looked like they would sooner stick pins in their eyes than be seen talking to me. My phone suddenly beeped, offering a welcome distraction from my increasingly depressing thoughts.

'All right, posh bird!' I heard a voice say before I could read the new text.

I spun around, startled. A rush of adrenalin hit my stomach. It was the girl from my English class, the one with the T-shirt, and her two friends. I thought Jessica had said her name was Janice. They were standing over by the skate park, propped up against a graffiti-covered wall. I noticed the word *Dove* again, with a picture of a little bird, like the one on the railway wall. It looked prettier up close. The same could not be said of the girl in front of me. Her narrow eyes squinted in the last bright rays of the day's sunshine. She had one foot up against the edge of the wall and she was drawing heavily on a cigarette. Her bubble-gum-pink track pants were emblazoned with the words *Sweet Couture* and her brazen T-shirt, partly hidden by a zip-up grey hoodie, tempted me to stare again.

'On your way home?' she asked. Although this was a perfectly reasonable question, I suddenly felt like running as fast as possible in the opposite direction. 'What's the matter,' she went on, barely giving me time to respond, 'don't you want to talk to me?' Her voice had a malevolent ring to it.

'Yes, er, no. Yes, I'm on my way home,' I stuttered. Part of me wanted to run like the wind, yet I found myself rooted to the concrete beneath me, terrified to move.

'Where's home then?' she said, continuing to look me up and down as she blew smoke from her mouth and chewed gum simultaneously.

I wanted to say Embers, just to totally flummox her,

but instead gestured pathetically behind me. 'I live on Erwine Street,' I managed to croak.

She sniffed. 'Nice boots,' she said, her eyes settling at my feet. I was wearing a pair of grey suede ankle boots that I'd bought from Hotshop, a cool fashion boutique. Tave had a red pair and we often wore them together with our skinny black jeans tucked inside, back when she still wanted anything to do with me.

'Thanks,' I said, perking up a bit. Perhaps I had her wrong and she was trying to be nice after all.

'Did your dad nick them then?' she said, a sly smile spreading across her badly painted lips. The two girls next to her grinned too. I was confused.

'I bought them in Hotshop,' I explained. 'They do them in red too,' I said, trying to be helpful. 'I'm sure you could probably still get them . . . '

Janice started to laugh and then stopped abruptly. 'Are you taking the mick?' she asked, flicking her cigarette butt in my direction. It landed inches away from my feet. Blue curly smoke wafted up towards my face. Instinctively I felt the need to tread on it but was too scared to make any sudden moves.

'Is that what he's in the nick for, shoe theft? Because those boots you're wearing are criminal!' Janice collapsed into hysterical laughter, closely followed by her cackling comrades.

*Oh God.* She knew about Dad. Had Jessica blabbed that quickly?

'Oh yes, sir, no, sir, three bags full, sir. *I've* heard of William Blake. I am the rotten rose!' Janice was pulling a childish face, doing a silly (and somewhat inaccurate) impression of me. 'Think you're something special when all the time, your old man's a bloody criminal, banged up in jail somewhere!' She made the same hissing sound with her teeth that the boy in class had made earlier.

'It's the *sick* rose, actually,' I said, wishing I could catch the words in the air as they left my mouth and stuff them back in again.

Her two cronies gasped in shock, clearly horrified that I had dared to correct her.

Janice dropped her foot from the wall and began to walk towards me with, I noted, some defiance. 'Sorry, I didn't catch that. Can you repeat yourself?' Her voice had a really menacing resonance to it now. It would be a good time to run, I thought to myself, but the message didn't quite reach my shaking legs. 'What's he locked up for, eh? Murder? GBH? Rapist, is he?' Janice snarled, nastily.

I could feel tears beginning to prick the backs of my eyes. Please God, don't let me start crying, I thought desperately. She was invading my space now, so I took two steps back, straight into a tree stump behind me. I lost my footing and landed, plop, flat on my bum. The three girls fell about laughing as, humiliated, I quickly picked myself up.

'Hey, Janice,' said a voice behind me.

I turned and saw a boy in a hoodie riding a BMX bicycle straight towards us. I was too frightened to look at him properly, so I turned quickly back, my heart

thudding so fast I could hardly breathe. Another friend
of Janice's was the last thing I needed.

# Chapter 5

'Give it a rest, Janice,' said the boy on the bike. His voice was surprisingly soft, and I shivered with relief.

'All right, JJ,' Janice said, stepping back from me a little as she addressed him. 'Just having a *friendly* chat with the new girl about her old man – inside for murder, apparently.' She shot me a sarcastic smile.

I dusted the back of my jeans with my hands. 'Fraud,' I blurted out. 'He's in prison for fraud, *not* murder.' I wasn't sure where the courage to stand up for myself had come from, but I sensed that the presence of the soft-speaking boy had helped a little. Still, I wasn't feeling *that* brave and, convinced I was about to get beaten to a pulp for my outburst, I turned on my grey suede heels and began swiftly walking in the opposite direction along the canal, even though it was actually the *wrong* direction for home.

'Catch you later, jailbird!' Janice called after me. I thought I heard the boy saying something to her, but I was too far away to make out what it was.

When I felt sure they couldn't see me, I finally allowed the tears to flow. I kept walking and didn't look back, the sound of my heart beating amplified in my ears. After a few minutes, the thud in my chest began to settle a little and I slowed my pace, sensing that I was out of danger. I reached inside my bag to look for a tissue to wipe my face. It wouldn't do to let Mums see that I'd been crying, not on my first day at school. She had enough problems without having to take on mine as well, like how we were going to afford to pay the rent and buy food. The previous day I had heard her talking to my dad's solicitor on the phone. She had sounded worried, desperate even. 'But there must be *something* left, a little stash somewhere – *anything*. My reserves are running danger-ously low, Marcus. We need to get our hands on some money and fast . . .' There had been a pause and then I heard her say, 'Yes, yes, I suppose I *will* have to find a job.'

Poor Mums. The thought of having to go out to work must be terrifying for her. I mean, what would she *do*? She has never had a 'proper' job. Dad didn't want her to work when they got married and, when me and Cal came along, well, it wasn't even up for discussion that she wouldn't stay at home with us, even if she wasn't always at home, strictly speaking. Although my mother is intelligent, any ambitions she might've once had were kept at bay by endless all-day spa treatments and shopping marathons. She admitted herself that her biggest achievement in life (aside from having me and Cal) was getting her picture in society magazine, *Sophisticate*!

Perhaps *I* could get a job, I thought, as I continued to walk in the wrong direction. Forget school, forget A-levels and university. I could go and work in a big office in the city, wear smart pencil skirts and cropped jackets every day and be a secretary for a young, handsome go-getter lawyer-type or something. That way I could help shoulder some of the financial burden. Of course, the young, handsome lawyer-type would instantly fall in love with me (due to my inimitable sense of style and poise) and give me favourable pay rises over all the other secretaries, who would undoubtedly be dead jealous and . . .

I heard the sound of someone behind me. Holy crap! Janice and her cronies must have followed me! I quickened my pace, too terrified to turn round. I hunched my shoulders, waiting for them to pounce. Perhaps after the beating, they would push me in the canal! Leave me to float away. I wondered whether, if I were to float for long enough, I might end up in Oxshott.

'Hang about,' the voice said. The boy who had intervened with Janice was cycling alongside me. What did he want? I allowed myself to glance at him. I figured he was probably a little older than me. He was skinny-looking and a little dishevelled. His hair, mostly hidden beneath his hoodie, was fair, a sort of honey blond colour, and his eyes were spectacularly green. I wished I could see them better, not least to suss out whether he was friend or foe. The stubble on his chin suggested he had forgotten to shave that day and he was wearing a baggy red T-shirt and black skater pants with a wallet chain visible outside his right pocket. He had a kind of 'undone' appearance, his black bomber-style jacket slipping off his shoulders slightly, as if he'd got dressed in a hurry, and his trainers, bright white with three black stripes down the sides, looked brand new. I wondered if he might belong in a gang who went around mugging old ladies and joyriding. By rights I should have been scared of him, but there was a softness about him that instantly put me at ease.

'You're crying,' he said, twisting the handlebars on his bike in an attempt to keep his balance. He looked a little horrified, as boys tend to when they see a girl cry. I felt embarrassed.

'No I'm not,' I snapped, even though it was obvious.

He let go of the handlebars and handed me a tissue from his pocket, which was weird because he didn't strike me as the sort to carry tissues around with him. 'Thanks,' I sniffed, taking it.

He got off his bicycle and began pushing it alongside me. 'Don't worry 'bout her,' he said, tilting his head back in the direction of Janice and her cronies, 'she's all mouth, that one.' He pronounced 'mouth' like 'mouff'. 'Fancy a rollie?' he said, pulling a small gold packet and some cigarette papers from one of his many huge pockets.

'No thanks,' I said, still unsure whether to make direct eye contact, 'I don't smoke.'

'Course not,' he replied. 'Dirty habit anyway. Sign of inadequacy.'

The word 'inadequacy' sounded odd coming from his lips, as if it didn't quite fit. 'Dunno why I do it really,' he said, lighting the roll-up and taking a drag.

'Then why *do* you do it?' I asked, immediately realising how confrontational I sounded.

'Dunno really,' he shrugged. 'Boredom ... habit ... social conditioning ... '

It was not the answer I had expected. I took a chance and looked up, and saw his face properly for the first time. He had a broad smile and his teeth were even and almost Hollywood-white, unusual for a smoker, I thought. He was actually quite nice-looking, if a little scruffy round the edges.

'I'm giving it up soon anyway. Bad for your health. Besides, I can't afford it.' He took another drag and I noticed his paint-splattered fingers. Suddenly conscious of how I must look to him, blotchy-faced and mascara-stained, I ran my finger underneath my eyes.

'You're new round here,' he said, flicking his cigarette into the canal. A lone moorhen glided over to inspect it, only to swim off again almost immediately. 'I can tell by your accent.'

'Yes,' I squeaked, clearing my throat, 'it was my first day at Kinsmead Comprehensive today.'

'It didn't go too well, then?' He must have detected the despair in my voice.

I shook my head, unable to speak for fear I might burst into tears, like you do when you're upset and someone starts being nice to you.

'There's always tomorrow,' he said, his eyes catching mine fleetingly. 'And don't worry about that gob on legs, Janice. She's got a bit of a reputation but her bark's worse than her bite.' I wondered what he meant by 'reputation'. 'Got a right mouth on her though, let me tell ya. I can hear it four floors up,' he laughed.

'You live near each other then?' I asked, hoping I didn't sound as if I was prying.

'I live in Hamlet Tower, just over there,' he said, pointing in the direction of the building that blocks the sun from my window, 'on the twenty-second floor.'

'Oh,' I said, trying to keep any negativity out of my voice.

He raised an eyebrow.

'I hear it's the work of quite a well-respected architect – the building I mean.' (Note to self: must remember to thank Cal for useless pieces of trivia that can help diffuse difficult situations and are therefore use*ful*.)

'Yeah, if I ever meet the bloke, I'll be sure to shake his hand.' I felt myself flush hot with embarrassment. He was being sarcastic.

'I bet the view's pretty stunning,' I said, ignoring it.

'Yeah,' he laughed, 'that's what the estate agent said: "panoramic views of London – the best Housing Benefit can buy".' He was making fun of me again.

'Sorry,' he said, shaking his head, 'it's just that it's funny listening to you in your posh accent trying to be nice about where I live, when we both know it's a proper . . . well, it's not exactly a penthouse, is it?'

I didn't like to answer. I couldn't be sure whether he was laughing at me or with me and I desperately didn't want to offend him. Not since he'd been kind enough to stand up for me.

'I realise my accent is somewhat different to most people's round here,' I said, hoping to deflect the conversation away from Hamlet Tower.

'Somewhat,' he repeated, smiling. 'Listen, I don't mean to disrespect you. I think your accent is nice. Seriously I do. It's different to hear someone talking the Queen's proper English for a change. You must be from a well nice part of the world. . .'

I wasn't sure if it was a question or not. I treated it as one anyway.

'Oxshott,' I replied. It made me feel happy just to say the name. Perhaps if I said it enough times and clicked the heels of my boots together I might be magically transported back there, like Dorothy in *The Wizard of Oz:* 'There's no place like home.' 'It's a small village in Surrey, very green and open and beautiful,' I continued, and suddenly our surroundings seemed even greyer and even more claustrophobic.

'Must be difficult,' he said, gesturing around him, 'all this.'

'The sirens keep me awake at night,' I said, full of self-pity.

'You'll get used to them,' he said softly, his hand lightly brushing mine as it swung. I quickly folded my arms.

'So, got a name then?' he asked.

'Grace. Grace Foster-Bryce.' It suddenly sounded weird saying my own name aloud.

'JJ,' he said, 'aka Dove.' He held out his hand and I shook it. 'It's a pleasure to meet you GFB. Maybe see you around,' he said, as he got on his bike and cycled away without turning back to look at me.

I stood, rooted to the pavement, unsure what to make

of him and the whole encounter. I looked down at my hand and noticed a couple of tiny spots of red paint on my fingers. I blinked at them.

'Hello there,' an old lady said as she walked by. 'Nice to see a happy face for a change.' Funny, I hadn't even realised that I was smiling.

'Ah, darling, you're back.' Mums was standing in the kitchen doorway dressed in a silk kaftan top and slim black leggings. Next to her was a tall, thin man with a big, dark beard and glassy blue eyes that bulged out of his head. I hadn't the foggiest idea who he was.

'How was your first day at school?' Mums didn't give me time to respond. 'Darling, this is Mr Sergeyev. Boris Sergeyev,' she said smiling at him. 'He lives next door and he's from Russia. Isn't that marvellous?' Mums widened her eyes at me, urging me to be polite.

'Nice to meet you,' I said, holding my hand out.

He shook it vigorously. 'I am charmed, Miss Foster-Bryce. Enchanted. You are as beautiful as your mother,' he said in a thick Russian accent that made him sound like a baddie in a spy film.

Mums gave a little coy flutter of a laugh and put her hand up to her face. 'You're embarrassing me, Mr Sergeyev,' she said, clearly enjoying every minute. 'Gracie, Mr Sergeyev.'

'Boris, please,' the man interrupted.

Mums smiled at him. 'Gracie, *Boris* here has kindly agreed to have a look at our boiler. The damn thing has been playing up since we got here, hasn't it, darling?' She looked at me for affirmation. 'Hot water one minute, ice cold the next. Taking a shower is a bit like playing a game of Russian roulette!' She let out a snort of laughter. I cringed. She was being *so* embarrassing. I could've sworn that she was actually *flirting* with this odd-looking man. 'So how *was* school?' she asked, again.

'It was OK,' I lied. 'I think I'll get used to it.'

'Fabulous, darling,' she said. 'You must tell me all about it later.' I could see she wasn't really paying attention. 'Can I get you some tea while you're tinkering, Mr Sergeyev – sorry, *Boris*?'

I decided to leave them to it and made my way up the small flight of stairs to my boxroom bedroom. I flopped down on to the bed and shut my eyes. I could hear the muffled voices of Mums and the Russian downstairs. I wondered what they were talking about. Maybe she was telling Boris all about Dad and our subsequent fall from grace. I imagined the Russian watching her lipstick-red mouth intently as she spoke, her clipped accent fascinating and exciting him in equal measures, making his eyes bulge even further out of his head. A wild fantasy crossed my mind: perhaps Mums and the Russian might fall in love. It would all start with him fixing the boiler and finish with him mending her broken heart. Dad would only have himself to blame if that were to happen, I thought.

But if *anyone* deserved a little romance in their life right now it was me. It had been ages since I'd had any kind of boy action. When you live somewhere as sleepy and self-contained as Oxshott for most of your life, it's easy to become boy-obsessed because that's pretty much all there is to do – well, that and ride horses. If I'm honest though, I was never really into boys quite as much I pretended to be to my friends. I thought they were OK and I enjoyed their attention when it (rarely) came my way. But my real love was acting and the theatre.

I was just five years old when I experienced the thrill of the stage for the first time. Dad took me to see *A Midsummer Night's Dream* at the open-air theatre in Regent's Park during the summer holidays. I was completely entranced, intoxicated by the passion, the colour and the drama of it all. Of course, I didn't have the foggiest idea of what the play was about (I was only five after all!) but it didn't matter; I was hooked. After that, I would always beg my parents to take me along to the theatre with them, though I loved it most when it was just me and Dad together. He would let me have a fizzy drink during the interval and we would discuss the play as if my opinion was of the utmost importance.

By the time I was thirteen, theatre was my number one interest (I loved acting as well by then, and had fantasies of my future career on stage). Film was a close second and my interest in boys came in a poor third. Thinking about it now though, the idea of meeting someone special suddenly seemed quite appealing. At the very least it would take my mind off all the recent hideousness. I sighed. The boys round this way certainly didn't look the sort to sweep you off your feet though – knock you off them, more like! The boy who had rescued me from Janice had seemed quite friendly, though, even if he did smoke and live on that rough-looking Hamlet estate. I wondered what the initials JJ stood for. James Johnson? John Jamison? Joe Jackson? Jeremiah Jenkins? Maybe, if I ever saw him again, I would have the courage to ask.

# chapter 6

♥

I dragged myself up from the bed and padded over to the window. I'd spent a couple of hours in my bedroom trying to make sense of the homework I'd been given that day, but tiredness had got the better of me. It was starting to get dark now and the lights from Hamlet Tower illuminated the sky. I wondered which one of the hundreds of flats JJ might live in. I was sure he had said it was the twenty-second floor. I tried to count from the bottom up, but it was almost impossible in the near dark. A train clattered past, its blaring horn still startling me, even after two weeks of hearing it several times a day. I watched its lights disappear into the distance, then something caught my eye on the wall beyond the tracks. Next to the bird graffiti was a single word: *Dove*.

'My name's JJ, aka Dove.' Was JJ the artist behind the graffiti? Perhaps that would explain the paint on his hands. A flutter of excitement tickled my stomach although I wasn't quite sure why.

I could hear Cal still watching the History Channel in his bedroom next door. The sound of guns and explosions penetrated the wafer-thin wall between us. I remembered that my phone had beeped earlier, and was surprised to see that the message was from Legs. I lay on the bed to read it.

*Hi Grace, hope ur cool. How's life in London? Am off 2 Dubai with the parents this wknd. Shld b fun! P'raps we can meet up when I'm back? Love Legs X*

I immediately texted her back.

*GR8 2 hear from u! London sucks and I miss u all terribly. Wld love 2 c u v v soon. Call me when ur back from Dubai. Have fun in the sun! Love G xx*

I tried not to feel jealous as I imagined Legs sunning herself on a Dubai beach surrounded by crystal blue waters. While she was persuading her father to splash loads of cash in all the local designer boutiques, I would be mooching around on my own, flat broke, or stuck inside my boxroom bedroom studying. At least she had thought of me enough to send a text. Perhaps we really would meet up when she was back, and I could catch up on all the Oakwood gossip. Maybe it would never be quite as it was before but we could still be friends, couldn't we? I held the thought in my head for a moment, hopeful.

There was a knock at the door. 'Only me, chickadee,' Mums said in a singsong, happy voice. I rolled my eyes. I wasn't sure I could stomach any of her forced saccharine conversation after the day I'd had. 'Can I come in?' She sat down on the bed next to me. 'You'll be relieved to know that Boris has managed to mend the boiler!' she squealed, excitedly. 'Stopcock or something. So, as he's saved us a ridiculous amount of money by not having to call out a plumber, I've invited him to dinner on Friday night.' She glanced quickly at me to see my reaction. 'That's all right with you isn't it, darling?'

'But you can't cook,' I said, leaning up on my elbow and propping up my head with my hand.

'I can!' she shot back defensively. 'I'll have you know Mrs Hardcastle, my old cookery teacher, once said my pineapple upside-down cake was the best thing she'd tasted in a decade!' I shot her a look of disbelief. 'It's true!' she insisted. 'I think I could've made quite an accomplished cook if we hadn't had Fabienne to do it all for us.'

We were both silent for a moment as we remembered our wonderful housekeeper. Fabienne had been with our family since Cal and I were very little. A warm, smiley French woman, she was like a second mother to us, cooking, cleaning, taking us to and from school and for days out when my parents were busy (which was most of the time), and it was Fabienne who had taught me the few domestic skills I had ever acquired. Sometimes I wondered if she had been more like a mother to me than my own mum had. We certainly seemed to spend more time with her, that's for sure. It had broken our hearts to have to say goodbye to her and Max when we left Embers, even though we all made a pledge to stay in touch.

'I'm sure it'll be a while before I get anywhere near Fabienne's standard,' continued Mums, 'but we can't live on microwave dinners and beans forever, can we, kitten? Far too taxing on the skin!' She patted her face. 'I'm sure I can rustle up a goulash or something. She'll have left us an old recipe book somewhere . . . maybe you'll give me a hand?' She looked at me hopefully. 'Anyway, Boris seems like a very nice chap and it'll be beneficial to have a handyman around the place to help change light-bulbs and such, especially now that we don't have anyone to do it for us . . . ' Her smile waned a little. 'So, darling,' she changed the subject quickly, 'school! Do tell all.' She clasped her hands together as if I was just about to impart the most exciting piece of news she'd ever heard in her life.

'Not much to tell, really.' I shrugged despondently.

'Oh come on, Gracie,' she said, mock frowning. 'What are your tutors like? Fellow students, common room . . .'

'Put it this way,' I said, 'it's no Oakwood.'

Mums lowered her eyes sadly. (Note to self: must remember that lying is not always such a bad thing.) Why did she always have to push? All she really wanted to hear was that everything was 'super' even when we both knew it was anything but. The faint sound of gunfire coming from Cal's room filled the silence between us.

'Mums,' I finally said, 'what are we going to do for money?'

She looked up at me with her deep brown eyes that I wished I had inherited, rather than her nose.

'I told you, Grace,' she said, her voice tight, 'you mustn't worry about all that. You just concentrate on your studies and leave the finances up to me.'

But I couldn't help worrying and I could tell by the way she was twisting the toggle on the mohair cardigan she was now wearing that she was worried too.

'I could always leave school and find a job in the City,' I offered. It had seemed like quite an exciting prospect when I had been thinking about it earlier.

'Good grief, Grace,' she said, sitting up straight. 'I will absolutely not hear anything of the sort. Dad and I paid extremely good money to give you a good, solid education and make sure you have the best possible chance of going on to university. I'll not have you throw it all away by going to work in some . . . office!' She looked at me, outraged.

'OK, OK,' I said quickly, not wanting the conversation to escalate into a fully-fledged row. I figured now was probably not the best time to mention my drama college ambitions. I wondered if there would ever be a good time.

Mum didn't exactly slam the door behind her as she left, but then again she didn't close it quietly either. Talking to her had made me feel even more alone. I longed to pour my heart out to someone who would understand.

Leaning over to switch the bedside lamp on, I caught sight of the letter. I held the velvety smooth envelope in my hand – Dad always used the finest quality notepaper – and looked at the familiar, calligraphic scrawl in black ink on the front. He had such beautiful handwriting. I had always tried to copy it but could never get the ys and gs right, even with the help of the expensive calligraphy pens he used to buy me. I stared at the envelope for a few minutes before ripping it to shreds and throwing it in the bin. Then I painted my toenails a bright, defiant red and went to bed.

* * *

'God, are you OK, Grace? You look like you're in pain!'

It was the next day and I was sitting on the bench in the playground eating my lunch alone like a total saddo, when I saw Jessica striding towards me purposefully.

As well as worrying about our increasing poverty, if me and Tave would ever speak again, whether Mums would run off with the Russian and if it was healthy for Cal to be so interested in war, I had spent some of last night thinking about what I would say to Jessica when I next saw her. I had decided upon the grand sum of 'nothing'. I would ignore her. What was the point in getting into an argument when I only had myself to blame?

'What's up with you?' Jessica said, wrinkling her brow. I didn't answer.

'It can't be *so* bad that you can't talk, surely!' she said in that am-I-joking-or-not kind of way that she does.

'Thanks,' I said with all the sarcasm I could muster.

'What for?' Jessica said, her face puzzled.

'For telling Janice that my father's in prison,' I said. 'The whole school probably knows by now and my little brother will no doubt be picked on as a result. You promised me!' I started walking away, and was nearly hit by a bag some Year Six boys were throwing around.

'Hey hang about,' Jessica said, indignant. 'I didn't breathe a word to anyone about your . . . well, you know . . . I swear!' She pushed her glasses back up her nose as she trotted alongside me.

'So how come that Janice girl knows then?' I asked.

'I have no idea, but I can assure you that she didn't

hear it from me! She'd be the last person I'd tell any juicy gossip to,' she said, quickly adding, 'not that the fact that your dad's in prison is juicy gossip, obviously.'

I looked at her face – it was a curious mix of outrage and panic.

'Are you *sure* you didn't breathe a word to anyone?' I said, unsure whether to believe her or not.

'I absolutely cross my heart and hope to die a long, slow and painful death from which I would never recover.' She held her hands up to protest her innocence.

'It would be impossible for you to recover from a slow and painful death,' I said, trying not to smile.

'Smart arse,' she said, and we both giggled a little uncomfortably. 'You know, it might not be such a bad thing if people think your dad's some hardened criminal anyway,' she said, evidently trying to look on the bright side. 'Round here, that sort of thing brings you kudos. Besides, we'll sort out anyone who might bully your little bro . . . or anyone that gives you any aggro too for that matter.' She linked her arm in mine and gave it a reassuring tug.

'Thanks,' I said, this time without a hint of sarcasm, as we walked past a scary-looking group of girls leaning against the railings with their arms folded.

'Anyway, cheer up,' Jessica said. 'The reason I was coming to find you in the first place was to invite you to a party at Hamlet Tower on Friday night. Shelly Dacre's mum has bogged off to Tenerife for a week with her toy boy so Shelly's got the place to herself. It'll be a laugh. You should come. Meet more people, circulate a bit, let everyone know you're not some stuck-up cow with a silver spoon in her gob. What do you say?'

'Well, seeing as though you put it so *nicely*, how can I refuse?' I said.

'Jolly smashing, stuff, what!' she said, nudging me with her elbow. I tried not to laugh but couldn't help myself.

'Will Janice be there?' I found myself asking.

'Probably, but don't worry about her. I'll be there and, if she so much as looks at you funny, I'll put washing-up liquid in her drink!' Jessica said defiantly. I appreciated her reassurance. 'So, are you going to come or not?'

'Maybe,' I said.

'*Definitely* maybe or *maybe* maybe?' Jessica asked.

'Maybe,' I repeated, feeling simultaneously chuffed and defeated. Mums would never let me go to a party on Hamlet estate. Would she?

# Chapter 7

♥

'Thank goodness you're back,' Mums said the minute I walked through the kitchen door that evening. She was wearing a blue stripy apron and had patches of what looked like flour in her hair.

'What on earth is that awful pong?' I asked, putting my hand up to my face. It smelled as if someone had set fire to the chairs.

'Oh yes, that's right, kick a dog when it's down, why don't you?' she said, only half joking. 'I've been having a trial run with this goulash nonsense for the stupid dinner party on Friday. All was going quite well until the phone rang and I clean forgot I had left the pan in the oven. What a complete ninnie. Look,' she held up a charred pan, 'it's burnt to a cinder.'

Dinner party. Friday. I had totally forgotten all about it. I smacked my forehead. 'Oh Mums, I'm so sorry but I don't think I'll be here for the dinner party thing after all,' I said, wincing in anticipation of her reaction. 'I've been invited to another party you see.'

She stopped attempting to scrape the black bits from the bottom of the pan and looked up at me.

'Oh darling, that is marvellous news,' she beamed. 'You see, you've only been here for five minutes and already you're in social demand! And you were worried about not fitting in! So, where is this party then and what's it in aid of?'

'A girl I've met at school called Jessica invited me and, er, I think it's a birthday party,' I said, unable to tell her the whole truth.

'Well, so long as it's nowhere near that dreadful estate over the railway line,' she said. 'I don't want you setting foot anywhere near that awful place.' She glanced at me fleetingly. 'I've seen the kids hanging out around there – delinquents the lot of them. Probably all on drugs. And the language! Oh! It's no place for people like us, Gracie. I don't want you mixing with their sort.'

'And what sort is that?' I asked, indignant. 'Criminals and poor people? Because, if that's the case, I should feel right at home, shouldn't I?'

Mums shot round and glared at me, but her anger soon dissipated into hurt. Oh God. I hated it when she did that. It was easy to be angry with her when she was angry too, but that injured look . . .

'I only want to protect you,' she bristled, dabbing the sides of her eyes with the corner of her apron. 'Is it so wrong of me to want to keep you away from a place like that?'

'Of course not,' I said, feeling guilty.

'And I really could use some help on Friday.'

I glanced at the blackened, burnt-out pan and bit my lip. 'But Mums,' I protested, 'you said you wanted me to fit in and make new friends. Somehow I don't think I'll be invited to many alfresco balls out here, do you?'

'Oh Gracie,' she said, exasperated, 'of course I want

you to make new friends and be happy. But we'll never fit in round here and, quite frankly, I hope we never do. All this,' she gestured around her with the spoon in her hand, 'it's just temporary. Soon enough this will all be a distant memory.'

'It's just one party,' I said, sullenly. 'I'll be with Jessica and I promise not to go near that estate . . . '

Mums sighed. 'OK, Grace,' she said, tying her hair into a chignon and securing it with a clip. 'If you *really* want to go . . .'

I let out a little squeak of excitement and threw my arms around her. I wasn't quite sure why I wanted to go to this party so much. I knew I would feel uncomfortable and self-conscious and that Janice and her cronies would probably be there giving me the evil eye all night, yet I had this strange feeling of anticipation fluttering inside my stomach, the sort I imagine you get before you go on stage in front of thousands of people. 'Here,' I said, taking the spoon from Mums's hand with a smile. 'Let me help.'

She smiled back, and I couldn't tell who was the most grateful out of the two of us.

It turned out to be a week of discoveries. On Wednesday afternoon, I found out that Mr Dickins ran a weekly drama group after school but that the auditions had already taken place during the lunch break. The one thing that might have helped make Kinsmead bearable, and I had gone and missed my chance. I was so disappointed, I sat down on my bed when I got home that evening and cried.

Then on Thursday I realised that Mums had been trying to get a job without actually telling us. I knew this because I'd seen her wearing her Armani suit twice. She only ever wears it to go to formal lunches or events and I was pretty sure she hadn't been to either of those, so I guessed she must be going to interviews.

But my biggest discovery that week by far came on Friday, courtesy of my new friend Jessica. We'd been sitting together on the school bench picking at our sandwiches over lunch when I suddenly blurted out, 'Do you know a boy called JJ?'

Jessica stopped mid-bite of her ham sarnie. 'JJ? You mean Dove? The graffiti dude off Hamlet estate?'

'Yes, I think so,' I said.

'What about him?' She raised an eyebrow.

I shrugged. 'What's he like?'

'Ohh, about six foot, quite fit, wears a beanie a lot . . . '

'No, silly.' I nudged her. 'I mean, what's he *really* like?'

Jessica put her sandwich back in its plastic carton and looked at me seriously. 'He's got a bit of a reputation. Been in trouble with the old bill loads for spraying on walls and stuff.'

'Oh, right.' My heart sank to my shoes.

'My mum reckons it's all just vandalism, however much you dress it up, but, if you ask me, he's an awesome street artist. Really talented,' she said, nodding sagely. 'And totally cute, if you're into that kind of urban skater boy thing. He went to school here at Kinsmead, only I think he was chucked out, or he walked before his exams or something.'

'I see.' I had hoped that maybe JJ and I could be friends, but now that I knew of his reputation I wasn't so sure. Mums would have a fit if she knew I'd even spoken to him.

'Anyway, why do you want to know?' Jessica asked, a sly smile creeping across her face. 'Fancy him, do you?'

'No!' I shot back, a little too quickly to be convincing.

'You do!' she retorted. 'Oh my God! You want to snog him!'

'Jessica!' I half screamed. 'Don't be so childish!'

She giggled. 'Well you never know, he might be at Shelly Dacre's party tonight if you're lucky.'

'Yeah, and if I'm unlucky, that Janice girl and her friends will all be there, snarling at me like a pack of wolves ready to pounce,' I said, suddenly feeling miserable again.

Jessica shuffled a little closer towards me. 'Look, don't let that old cow intimidate you. You're better than that. And your sandwiches look better than mine, so swapsie one of your tuna and cucumber for my ham and cheese spread?'

I rolled my eyes and sighed, a suppressed smile getting the better of me as I handed her one of the sandwiches I had made for myself that morning.

'Here you go, Jessica.'

'Nice one,' she said, taking a large bite. 'Oh and Grace, call me Jess won't you? All my good friends do.'

'OK, Jess,' I said, suddenly feeling a little better.

I wrapped my big fake fur coat around me tightly to

combat the chilly September air and stepped into the lift, praying that it wouldn't break down. It wasn't the kind of place you would want to be trapped in for long.

I checked my phone.

*Flat 87, Hmlet Twrs, Westbrn Park, 9pm. C u there, square! Jess x*

I had hoped to meet up with Jess beforehand so that we could arrive at the party together, but she hadn't suggested it and I had been super-unassertive and not mentioned it either.

After what seemed like an age, the clunky lift juddered to a halt. I stepped out into the cold air and tried not to look down at the parked cars and the group of young kids who were shouting and throwing bricks and rubble into a skip full of rubbish below. The sound of a baby crying filled the air and I recognised the opening tune of a TV soap as I walked past the dimly lit windows. Human shadows moved behind shabby net curtains and the sound of a dog barking made me quicken my pace. My heart was racing so hard in my chest as I rang the bell of number eighty-seven that I thought I might keel over. Eventually, after the second buzz, the door swung open and a small girl in an aqua-blue tracksuit with her hair scraped back in a ponytail greeted me with a disdainful look. She was only just managing to restrain a large black dog which was barking furiously. 'Who are you?' she asked, yanking the deranged dog back by its collar.

'Hi, er, I'm Grace. Grace Foster-Bryce,' I stuttered nervously, offering her the family-sized box of Maltesers I had brought along with me as a gift. The dog was making a low growling noise now and baring its teeth at me.

''Ere, Shel,' she shouted behind her. 'Do you know this girl or what?'

The girl disappeared for a second and was replaced by another who was a year or two older but looked almost identical, except for a different colour tracksuit.

'You must be Shelly. Pleased to meet you,' I said, holding out my hand for her to shake it. She didn't take it. 'I'm a friend of Jessica's. She said to meet her here at nine.'

'You the posh girl?' she said, looking me up and down and then disappearing behind the door for a split second to talk to someone. I couldn't see who or hear what they were saying though because the music was far too loud.

'Come in,' she finally said without smiling.

I walked into what appeared to be a hallway full of people drinking from beer bottles, shouting and smoking. A sea of baseball caps bobbed up and down in time to the repetitive beats of the music and I noticed a couple slumped against a wall. The girl was almost falling over, her eyes rolling in her head as the boy tried to hold her up.

'She's mashed, mate,' I heard him say to another boy, 'proper out of it.'

It was warm inside the flat. Immediately I felt claustrophobic so I tried to find my way into a quieter room, somewhere I could sit down and catch my breath. I opened a door that led to a kitchenette – it was too small to be called a kitchen. I noticed the lino was covered in hundreds of brown marks which I realised were cigarette burns.

People were jostling for space, pulling cans out of the small fridge and pouring what looked like cider into plastic cups on the tiny work surface. The whole place smelled of boiled cabbage and sweat. I hid behind the kitchenette door, trying to look inconspicuous, which was tricky in a great big fluffy coat with a box of Maltesers in my uncontrollably shaky hand. People were beginning to stare at me. *Where was Jessica?* I tried not to think about the fact that I was all alone in a stranger's flat on a rough council estate with a heap of scary-looking people I didn't know. Worse still, I saw that most of the girls were either wearing jeans or track pants and T-shirts – not a dress in sight. I began to wish I had stayed at home with Mums and the Russian now. I scanned the small room again in the hope that I might see JJ and have a familiar face to talk to. I felt strangely deflated when I couldn't see him.

'Hey! Grace! Grace!' I heard Jess shout as she tried to fight her way through the throng. 'You made it then!' She was beaming at me brightly.

'I want to go home,' I said pathetically, the words tripping off my tongue before I could stop them. Her face dropped.

'Don't be daft, you've only just got here,' she said. I saw that she was wearing a little butterfly clip in her hair that matched her pink top, which she was wearing with baggy jeans and trainers. 'Take your coat off and let's get a drink,' she said.

'Actually, Jess, I'm still a little chilly,' I lied as she took my arm and led me back into the kitchenette. Ridiculously overdressed in my black chiffon dress with the spaghetti straps and gold kitten-heel sandals, I decided it was best I kept my coat on. I would just have to boil like an egg.

'This is Grace Foster-Bryce,' Jessica said, introducing me to Shelly properly. 'She's new at Kinsmead.'

'We've already met,' Shelly mumbled, giving me an uninterested look. 'Bring any drink with you?'

'Er, no,' I said, panicking. She glanced at the box of Maltesers I was now trying to hide behind my back. I wondered if, like me, they too were beginning to melt. Shelly looked at Jessica and made a circular movement with her finger at the side of her head as if to say I was completely mad. How embarrassing. I might as well have turned up with jelly and ice cream! Back in Oxshott, the etiquette was that if you went to a friend's gathering you always bought a little gift for the host – chocolates or flowers or something. I sensed a bottle of Mums's Campari might've gone down better!

'You look nice,' I said to Jessica, trying to disguise my embarrassment.

'You look *hot*,' she replied. 'And I mean in the over-heated sense. Take your coat off, you loon; you're going red in the face.' She was right – my skin was beginning to prickle and burn. Jessica began yanking my coat open in an attempt to pull if from my shoulders. I struggled.

'Check it out,' a boy said as Jessica finally managed to prise it from me. 'Where are you off to, the Ritz?' He was pointing at me and pulling a face.

'She's the posh girl, innit,' said a girl in a brown zip-up jacket and jeans who I'd never seen before. 'Her dad's in the clink or something, so I heard.' They were talking about me right in front of my face as if I wasn't there.

'What the hell are you wearing?' I heard a familiar voice say. 'Planning on meeting Mummy and Daddy at the opera later or something, yah?' It was Janice Brady flanked by her motley crew. 'Oops, silly me,' she said, holding her hand up to her forehead. 'Course, Daddy can't get to the opera these days can he? Too busy sewing mail bags.' Everyone was looking at me.

'Shut up, Janice,' Jessica muttered under her breath.

'Might've known you two would buddy up,' Janice snorted, 'Freaky Beaky and the posho. Nice combo.'

Jessica flashed Janice a sarcastic smile but I sensed that, like me, she was scared of her.

'You've got no business here,' Janice said. 'We don't like your sort looking down their stuck-up noses at us. Who invited you anyway?'

'I did,' Jess said, defiantly. Janice gave her a sideways glance before pushing past us, 'accidentally' emptying the contents of her plastic cup all over me as she went.

'Oops,' she said in a fake butter-wouldn't-t-melt voice, 'terribly sorry, old bean.' Her cronies cackled as I stood there in shock, cider dripping down my dress and coat and on to the floor.

'Come on, Grace, let's go. There's suddenly a *very* bad smell in this room,' Jess said, grabbing me by the arm.

'Listen, Jess,' I said, apologetically as we slunk off to

the bathroom in search of something to mop up the mess. 'I think I'd better go home. Janice is right; I'm not welcome here.' I felt bad that Jess was getting grief on my account. I didn't want to be a burden. Besides, I looked even more ridiculous now and I smelled horrible. It was best all round if I left her to hang out with her other friends and have a good time.

'It won't always be like this you know, Grace,' Jess said, giving me a sympathetic look. 'Give it time.'

'You sound just like my mother,' I said.

'Well,' she said, sucking air in between her teeth, 'you know what they say: Mums are always right!'

'Yeah,' I replied, 'a RIGHT pain in the bum!'

'You've stopped dripping,' Jess said, as she finished wiping my coat, 'so at least you can make a glamorous exit if you insist on leaving.'

'Yeah, right!' I said, but shot her a rueful smile as we both squeezed back out into the crowded hallway. 'I'll see you then.' Studiously looking down at the dirty carpet, I made my way to the front door and out on to the chilly walkway and back into the lift.

He was standing there as the lift doors finally opened. I quickly pretended I was checking my phone to avoid having to make eye contact with him.

'Hi mate,' JJ said, looking surprised to see me, 'where are you off to?'

# Chapter 8

'I'm going home,' I said, my voice a tad shaky. JJ was wearing dark jeans, a black bomber jacket, and white trainers with the laces undone. With his hood down, I could see that his blond hair was somewhere in between short and long. He didn't look much like a criminal. But then again, I above all people should know that someone doesn't actually have to wear a stripy vest and carry a swag bag to be one.

'What, all the way to Oxshott?' he joked. I was amazed that he'd remembered where I was from.

'I wish,' I said, a little unnerved.

'I wouldn't flash that phone around if I were you,' he said, nodding at my mobile. 'It's not a good idea round here.'

'Oh,' I said, flipping it shut and putting it back in my pocket.

'You're not going to the party then?' he asked, putting his foot in front of the lift door to prevent it from closing. My heart began thudding underneath my ribs.

'Oh, been there, done that, got a drink poured over me,' I said, nonchalantly, trying to make light of the whole horrible event.

'So that's why you smell like a wino, is it? Janice Brady have anything to do with it, by any chance?' I nodded.

He was being nice to me again. I hoped it wouldn't make me cry like last time. 'Well, hang about then,' he said, as I moved to step out from the lift, 'I'll walk with you.'

'No, really,' I said quickly. 'It's fine. I'd rather walk alone if you don't mind.' I was still a little wary of him. After all, Jess had told me all about his shady past.

'Well, actually, I *do* mind,' he said, pretending to be affronted. At least I think he was pretending. 'Besides, you don't want to be walking back through the estate at this time of the night on your Jack Jones, especially with that fancy mobile.'

A conversation was the last thing I wanted right now, looking ridiculous, my coat smelling like a wet dog – an *alcoholic* wet dog – but I found myself asking, 'Is that what JJ stands for then, Jack Jones?'

He laughed. 'It stands for Jay. Jay Jones.'

'Oh,' I said, beginning to walk on. 'No relation to Jack, then?'

He quickly followed. 'No. Although I once had a distant uncle called Jack,' he laughed, 'Bit of a ladies' man, by all accounts. Not that I'm . . . well, anyway, I reckon I should walk with you,' he said, striding alongside me.

I had to admit I was not exactly relishing the idea of walking home alone in the dark and he did have this rather approachable manner about him. 'OK,' I agreed. 'If you're sure.'

We made off in the direction of Sometime Place. I wrapped my damp coat around me tightly as I felt the first few drops of oncoming rain. There was an uncomfortable silence between us as we walked down the dimly lit path together.

'This place has an identity crisis,' I said, trying to think of something to say. 'It's a park that thinks it's a garden, or maybe it's a garden that thinks it's a park. What do you think?' I asked nervously, hoping he wouldn't think I was a complete mental case who worried about that sort of thing.

He looked at me in mild amusement. 'Hmmm,' he pondered. 'You're right. It ain't a park nor a garden but something in between. It's a pardon.'

I laughed. 'Yes,' I smiled. 'A pardon.' I liked that.

'I used to play here all the time as a kid,' he said. 'That skate park was like a second home to me and my brothers.'

'You have brothers?'

'Two,' he said, adding, 'and three sisters.'

'There's six of you!' I said, a little stunned.

'Seven including my ma,' he said. I tried to imagine it. Seven human beings crammed like sardines in one of those tiny flats, all on top of each other, unable to find their own quiet space. I dreaded to think what it must be like in the mornings, trying to get a turn in the bathroom.

'And you?' he asked.

'Oh, there's just me and my brother, Cal,' I said. 'I'm the eldest.'

'Me too,' he said. I detected a hint of strain in his voice, as if being the eldest in his family brought with it great pressure and responsibility. 'Sorry about your coat,' he said, changing the subject. 'I swear I'll have words with Janice about it, tell her to back off.'

'Oh no, please don't,' I said, sounding more desperate than I wanted to. I was hoping Janice wouldn't hear about him walking me home. Something in the way she'd acted around him suggested she had a bit of a thing for him and it would only give her more reason to hate me. 'It's fine, really. Anyway,' I laughed, 'I'm more concerned over what Mums will say when I arrive home stinking like an old wino!'

'I'll ask my ma to clean it for you, if you like,' he offered.

'No. Well, thanks, that's awfully kind of you and everything, but it's fine.' I said, wrapping the coat around me tightly.

'I promise to give it back!' he said defensively. 'Not everyone who lives on a council estate is a thief, you know!'

'Of course!' I said, careful to keep the tone of the conversation breezy. I didn't want to give him any reason to turn nasty on me.

'You're not scared of me, are you?' he asked, clearly sensing my apprehension.

'Of course not,' I lied.

He continued to smile at me a little strangely, exposing a small dimple on his left cheek. 'You've heard stuff about me, haven't you?' he said. 'Bad stuff.'

'Bad stuff?' I echoed, feigning ignorance.

'That I've been in trouble with the cops and that . . .'

'Oh, that,' I said, casually as if I knew plenty of people who'd had brushes with the law.

'It was a long time ago now. I was just a kid. Besides,

all artists must suffer for their work,' he said with a certain amount of irony.

'So you're an artist then?' I had to admit I was intrigued.

'Of sorts,' he replied. 'Not the type of artist you're thinking of though.'

'And what type of artist am I thinking of?' I said, mildly offended that he might suppose to know what I was thinking.

'Oh, you know, them fancy ones, Picasso and Rembrand and that.'

'It's Rembrand*t*,' I said, then immediately wished I hadn't.

'Yeah, that dude too,' he nodded. 'I'm more of a street artist though, an urban impressionist, if you like,' he said with a hint of pride.

'But isn't it illegal,' I asked, 'spraying on walls and stuff?'

'Well, yeah,' he said, 'I try to use designated areas, where it's legal, but it's not always possible. It's not like I go spraying on people's houses or front doors or anything. I choose places that need brightening up, places my art can bring colour and life to – like the skate park or the railway walls.'

'The railway?' I said, suddenly remembering the picture of the bird I could see from my boxroom bedroom. 'Did you paint the dove on the wall down there?'

'Yeah,' he nodded, smiling. 'That was me.'

'I can see it from my bedroom window,' I said.

'You can?' he asked, suddenly sounding a little bashful.

'Why did you choose to paint a dove?' I was curious. It didn't seem to fit with his cool skater-boy image.

'Well,' he said, sucking his breath in as if it was going to be a long story, 'Ma nicknamed me Dove when I was little. She reckons her and my old man never fought as much whenever I was around, that I had this way about me that calms other people. So it just kind of stuck. I like it because a dove represents peace. And we could all do with a little bit more of that in this world, couldn't we?'

'Yes,' I said, touched that he even seemed to care about such things. 'Isn't it awfully dangerous though,' I asked, 'having to stand that close to the railway tracks. It must be terrifying with all those trains whizzing past.'

'S'pose,' he said, shrugging. 'It's no big deal. I've spent my life dodging trains. You get used to it after a while, like most things.' I wondered if he was trying to suggest I would get used to my new life round here too.

'I didn't realise there were designated areas for graffiti – sorry, *street art*,' I said, a little surprised. There was no graffiti in Oxshott, not even down by the railway, and certainly no places where you might actually be *allowed* to do it.

'Oh yeah,' he said, 'me and few other graffers are going to do a piece next Friday up in Ladbroke Grove by the SmartSave car park. You can come and watch if you like,' he added casually.

I was too unsure to say yes, but then again I didn't want to say no either, so I just nodded.

'Which art college did you attend?' I asked.

'Are you kidding?' he laughed. 'Left school as soon as I could last year – hated it. Couldn't be bothered with all that college crap either.'

Underneath the bravado, though, I was sure I detected a hint of regret in his voice.

'I'd like to make a proper living from it one day – I already get the odd commission now and again,' he said, as if to make it clear he wasn't a total loser. 'I did the newsagent shop wall up near the bus garage. Have you seen it? The one with the pictures of the grannies and Rastas and skate punks and mums with pushchairs, all waiting for the bus? It's supposed to represent the community; black and white, young and old – everyone living together.' He seemed quite proud of it.

'No, I haven't. You must be very talented,' I remarked.

'Well, anyway,' he said, going a little shy again, 'I do some odd jobs on building sites too. Cash in hand, you know, bricklaying and that kind of stuff.' He kicked a cola can that was in his path. I watched it clatter into the gutter along with the rest of them. 'I don't enjoy it but . . . well, I need the money, don't I?'

There was a slight resignation in his voice, and I wondered if he had once had hopes and dreams for himself and deep down was afraid he might never realise them. A pang of sadness squeezed my chest. 'Still,' he continued, perking up, 'you've got to play the hand that you're dealt, haven't you? Besides, I have a few aces up my sleeve.' He winked at me and I felt myself blush.

'My parents are hoping I will become a lawyer or doctor or something – they haven't quite made up their minds yet,' I said, the bitterness in my own voice surprising me.

'Wow, a doctor or a lawyer, huh? A proper job,' he said, impressed.

'But really I want to be an actor,' I confessed. 'I would never tell my parents that though.'

'Why not?' he asked, meeting my gaze intently.

'Well, I suppose they just want me to have a good, solid career – something stable. They don't view acting as a real job,' I said, thinking how easy it was talking to him.

We walked past a cluster of people as we left Sometime Place.

'All right, Dove,' a boy in a checked baseball hat said, giving JJ a high five. 'How's it going, man? You not graffing tonight?'

'Nah mate,' said JJ, 'next weekend.'

'You going to Shelly Dacre's later?' the boy asked, looking me up and down.

'Maybe later,' JJ said.

'Sound. Who's this then?' He nodded at me.

'Mate of Jess's,' JJ said quickly. 'Listen man, got to split. Laters.'

I was a little hurt that he didn't seem to want to introduce me to his friend and that he'd referred to me as Jess's friend, as if to make the point that I wasn't his. But I didn't say anything.

We walked in silence for a bit and then, as we approached Goldborne Road, he turned to me and said quietly, 'I was sorry to hear about your dad.'

I didn't look at him. 'I bet everyone knows by now,' I

said, tight-lipped. I really didn't want to talk about it, spoil a perfectly pleasant, if a touch soggy, walk home.

'You know what it's like round here,' he said softly. 'Gossip spreads like butter on a hot day.'

'That's just it, though,' I said, feeling the emotion rise up through my chest. 'I *don't* know what it's like round here. And what's more, I wish I didn't *have* to know.'

He blinked at me, a little surprised by my sudden outburst.

'I miss everything about my home so much,' I wailed, unable to stop myself, even though I knew I sounded like a spoilt little princess. 'My school, my friends and Piccalilli.'

'Piccalilli? Isn't that the stuff you put in sandwiches at Christmas?' He furrowed his brow. 'Don't worry – the corner shop sells it.'

'No, no,' I said, mildly irritated, 'Piccalilli is the name of a *horse*, a beautiful dapple-grey horse. I've had him since I was twelve years old,' I lowered my head, 'but because of my stupid father, Tabitha Higginbottom-big-bottom now owns him instead.'

'You named your horse after a pickle,' JJ said, amused. Annoyingly, I found myself smiling too.

'Yeah, so?' I said, defensively. 'I *like* piccalilli.'

'I'm more of a ketchup man, myself, it has to be said.'

We walked the last few steps up to the old red door of 146 Erwine Street in silence. I think he sensed he'd struck a nerve by bringing up Dad.

'I can see your house from my flat,' he said, looking behind him in the direction of the tower block and changing the subject.

'I'm surprised you can't see space from up there,' I said, not meaning it to sound as sarcastic as it did. 'Perhaps we can converse in Morse code by using our bedroom light switches,' I suggested, trying to make up for it.

'That's a cool idea,' he said. I think he actually meant it. 'Or you could always give me your number. It might be easier.'

Uh-oh. Dilemma time. One the one hand, I wanted to give him my phone number because he'd asked for it and I needed all the friends I could get right now. On the other hand, I didn't want him to think that I just gave my phone number out to any Tristram, Dominic and Henry who asked for it. And Mums would have ten hairy fits if she found out I'd given my digits to someone who lives on a council estate.

I gave it to him. After all, I'd lost everything else, why not my sanity?

I glanced up at my new/old house. I couldn't be sure, but I had that uncomfortable feeling that someone was watching us. I could've sworn there was curtain movement in the living room window.

'Well,' I said, looking down at my wet toes poking out from my gold sandals. 'Thanks so much for walking with me.'

'No worries, mate,' he said.

I turned to go up the steps that led to the shabby red door.

'Grace,' he said suddenly, as if he'd forgotten to tell me

something important. I turned round halfway up the steps to look back at him. 'You know, sometimes good people do bad things; it doesn't mean you should write them off as all bad.'

It was quite a profound thing to say, not least from someone wearing a hoodie. I wasn't sure if he was referring to the things he had done himself, to my dad, or even to Janice Brady – perhaps he meant all three. It was bizarre but I was suddenly possessed by an urge to run down the steps and hug him, to thank him for being kind; for not treating me like some kind of freak show and for listening to me sound off about how miserable I was in this horrid place. Instead, I simply said, 'See you around, JJ, er, Dove, er – what do I call you?'

'Anything you like,' he shrugged. 'Laters, Grace Foster-Bryce.'

As I closed the door behind me, I was struck by an odd feeling. Sometimes people come into your life and you know instinctively that they are meant to be there for a reason. I didn't know for what reason JJ had come into mine, only that I was very glad he had.

# Chapter 9

The dinner party had been a complete disaster, culinary-wise. Mums, having given up on the goulash idea after her third failed attempt, had decided to make a pie instead, but she had clean forgotten to turn the oven on, and, by the time she realised this small but essential fact, it was nearing nine o'clock. It was almost eleven p.m. before they sat down to eat.

'Poor thing,' Mums said of the Russian. 'He must have been half-starved.'

But she still seemed happier than usual the following morning, giving me more cause to wonder if perhaps she and Boris really might end up falling in love.

'You seem in a good mood,' I said as she stood with her back to me at the sink. It was still odd to see her washing dishes. 'Any particular reason?' I asked with a wry smile. 'Don't suppose it has anything to do with a certain hairy Russian who lives next door, hmmm? Come on, Mums, you can tell me, don't be bashful.'

Mums stopped what she was doing and turned round to face me. 'How could you even think such things, Grace?' she said, clearly appalled. My face dropped. 'I am married to your father. You remember him, don't you?' My sarcasm problem was clearly hereditary.

'Oh, *that* father,' I replied, facetiously. 'Anyway, I was just joking,' I sniffed.

Mums sighed as she began slowly peeling off the rubber gloves she was wearing. 'How was the party?' she said, swiftly changing the subject. 'I saw you . . . *heard* you come in but you went straight upstairs to bed. Did it all go OK?'

'Yes,' I lied. 'It was fun I suppose.'

'Splendid. I'm glad.' She glanced at me tentatively. I could tell she was about to say something important, because she had that slight frown on her face that only ever appears when she's either about to tell me off or ask me about school. Whichever it was, I sensed now was not a good time to tell her I planned to go out the following Friday night and watch my new friend, JJ, spray graffiti on the wall by SmartSave's car park.

'You haven't been anywhere near that council estate, have you, darling?' she asked, folding a tea towel carefully. 'You know I don't want you hanging around that place. And that includes fraternising with anyone who lives there. Start mixing with their sort and you can kiss goodbye to any hope of a decent future. You'll be pushing a second-hand pram and queuing up for your housing benefit wearing a cheap towelling leisure suit before you can say, "DSS".'

I gasped in horror. 'Mums!'

'Well, it's true, darling,' she snorted. 'I've seen those girls mooching around, looking as though they need a decent bath, a brood of babies in tow and the boys with them, all scruffy and work-shy, smoking and drinking and swearing. I tell you, mix with life's losers and you will become one yourself.'

I was momentarily speechless. I couldn't believe how judgemental she was being. How could she make such sweeping generalisations, when she didn't even know anyone from Hamlet estate? I crossed my fingers behind my back.

'I was with Jess, anyway,' I said, pretending to read the headlines of *The Times* on the kitchen table.

Her face softened a bit. 'So that boy, the one you were with last night, he's not from that estate then?'

A-ha! So she *had* been watching me! I didn't want to lie to her, but just recently she had become so interested in my social life that it was hard not to. Back in Oxshott, she was always far too busy with her own social life to worry about mine. So long as I got good grades and was home on time, I could pretty much come and go as I pleased. Things were different now though and, annoyingly, she had begun to check up on me.

'What if he is?' I said, playing devil's advocate. 'Would it be *so* terrible?'

Mums took a sharp intake of breath. I could tell she was trying not to lose her temper.

'I did *ask* you not to hang around up there, Gracie, and now I am *telling* you. This is an important time in your life. You have exams looming and lots of hard work ahead of you. Nothing good will come of you spending time up there.'

'If you must know, he offered to walk me home,' I said. 'He was being a gentleman.'

'That's very commendable, darling,' she replied, 'but I mean it. You're not to hang around up there. I won't have years of expensive education go to waste just because we've had to come and live here . . . temporarily.'

I rolled my eyes as I stared at the newspaper. What a terrific snob! All this from someone who claims to be into left-wing politics! Mums had taught me to judge people as individuals and not by what they have or where they live. Now I realised that this only included people who lived in Oxshott (most of whom had varying degrees of wealth). What's more, she seemed to have forgotten that those were the very people who turned their backs on us the moment we had fallen from grace.

'OK,' I said, shrugging. It was easier just to agree with her. Besides, it wasn't as if I actually had any desire to hang out on Hamlet estate anyway . . . but I did hope to see JJ again. I sensed we could become good friends. There was something about him. Something unusual that I couldn't put my finger on, but it made me feel happy and warm inside whenever I thought about him. And he wasn't exactly *bad*-looking.

'Good, that's settled,' she nodded. 'Coffee, darling?' She poured me a cup from the cafetière.

I took a slurp. 'Eww. There's bits of coffee in this,' I said, pulling a face as I reached for the lone pain au chocolat sitting on a plate in the middle of the table. I noticed a visiting order from Altringham Prison next to it. Suddenly I had no appetite.

So that's why Mums was in such a good mood. She was going to see Dad.

'You didn't mention you were going to visit Dad,' I said, accusingly.

'I really don't know why this blasted thing isn't working properly,' Mums said, stooping down to inspect the cafetière and ignoring me. 'I mean, how hard can it be to make a decent cup of coffee?'

'Mums . . .' I said, prompting her.

'Perhaps there's a part missing or someth–'

'MUMS!' I screamed.

She stopped what she was doing and pulled up a chair resignedly. 'Yes. I am going to visit your father today,' she said quietly. 'I have to be there at three. I'll be getting the train as I don't think the old car will make it. It's on its last legs.'

'You never said,' I said, feeling oddly upset. Mums had visited Dad at least once every month since he'd been in prison. The first few times she had returned full of stories and anecdotes about how well Dad looked and how he was working in the library and had made friends. She made it sound like he was away at boarding school.

'I didn't mention it because I didn't think you would be interested,' she said. 'You never have been before.' She was searching my face, trying to gauge what I was thinking. 'Would you like me to give him a message, kitten?' she asked, her tone much softer. 'He would be over the moon if you did.'

I tried to think of something clever to say, a message that would instantly convey all my feelings in one sentence. But I realised such a sentence didn't exist. Instead, I found myself wondering what he might look like in his prison uniform. Smart and regal most probably. Dad could make a sackcloth look like it had been cut at Saville Row. A small smile crept across my face. I quickly erased it. 'No!' I snapped, standing up. 'No message. And by the way, I'm going over to Jessica's next Friday to do some studying. But don't worry. She doesn't live on *that* estate,' I said, as I flounced out of the room.

As if life hadn't been tough enough these last few weeks, I was now faced with the problem of what to wear to go and watch JJ and his mates spray graffiti on walls. I tried on the entire contents of my wardrobe (minus the ballgowns) twice, yet I still couldn't make up my mind. Nothing I owned seemed, well, *street* enough. Perhaps I should ask Jess for tips, I thought. Jess had squealed like a banshee when I told her that JJ had walked me home from the party.

'Oh my God, you two are *so* going to fall in love, get married and have lots of babies!' she gushed.

'Steady on,' I giggled, 'he only walked me home.'

'I'm telling you,' she said, unwavering, 'the Beakster is never wrong about these things. It's a sixth sense I have.'

'Really?' I said.

'Yup. I predicted that Lindsay Honeybon and Gareth Dudley would snog at Sabrina Matheson's sixteenth and they did – all night long!' she exclaimed proudly.

'Well, anyway, it's unlikely anything will ever happen with JJ and me,' I said, a little crestfallen.

'And why not?' Jessica demanded. 'It's perfect. The

good girl and the bad boy – it's like Danny Zucco and Sandra Dee from *Grease!*'

I sighed. 'I love that film. It's one of my all-time favourites, along with *Show Boat* – what a classic. Ava Gardner is just amazi–'

'Er, yeah, whatever,' Jess said, interrupting me.

'Anyway,' I continued, 'Mums would rather grow a beard than let me have anything to do with anyone from That Ghastly Estate. Besides, it's not like that. We're just friends.'

'Yeah, right, and I *enjoy* having periods and spots,' she sniggered.

I was in an especially good mood that Friday night. Aside from the fact that it was the end of a school week and the start of the weekend, I was feeling more hopeful than I had felt in ages, mainly, it has to be said, thanks to Mr Dickins.

'Ah Grace, yes, hang about for a moment, won't you?' he'd said as we dispersed after a double English period. 'Your essay.'

'Was everything OK with it, sir?' I enquired, a little nervously. I knew my mind had been elsewhere recently and I hoped it wasn't starting to have a bad effect on my schoolwork, as that would give Mums yet another reason to get on my case.

'Yes, yes, don't look so worried, he said reassuringly. 'However, I think you accidentally handed this in by mistake too.' He fiddled with a loose button on his shirt, as if *he* were the one who was embarrassed, and handed me a piece of paper.

I scanned the first few lines: *I would like to take this opportunity to thank my family, my friends and, of course, the academy . . .*

Oh Lordy! It was the Oscar acceptance speech I had written when I was about ten years old. How the hell had that got there?

'It was inside your work book, Grace,' Mr Dickins said. 'I read the first line and realised this was not meant for my eyes.' He smiled kindly.

Of course – what a complete idiot! I had been rifling around in one of my still-yet-to-unpack boxes last week when I was supposed to be doing my William Blake essay and had come across it. Lord only knows how, but I must've accidentally filed it with my work and handed it in to Mr Dickins – oh, the shame!

'I didn't realise you had aspirations to act, Grace,' he said, handing me the speech. 'You should have auditioned for a place in my drama club.'

I looked down at the floor, unable to meet his gaze. 'I would've liked to, sir,' I mumbled, 'only by the time I found out about it, all the places had been taken.'

'Right, *riiight*.' Mr Dickins stroked his chin understandingly. 'Well, it might be too late to join my drama workshop, but it's not too late to audition for a part in this year's school play – the great Shakespearean tragedy *Othello*. Anyone can come along – it's an open audition and the lead female part of Desdemona is still very much up for grabs.'

'Oh,' I said, my dashed hopes resurrected. 'I see.'

'Auditions are taking place next Thursday after school

at the youth centre – that's where we will be performing the play this year while maintenance work takes place in the main hall. Perhaps I'll see you there, Grace.' He gave me an encouraging smile.

'Yes, sir,' I said enthusiastically as I almost skipped out of the classroom, 'perhaps you will.'

I felt a little guilty for lying to Mums about going out with Jess and it was beginning to ruin my high. I had introduced Jess to Mums one morning when she had knocked for me on the way to school. Jess, a self-confessed expert in dealing with all things parent, had said all the right things in the right places. I could tell Mums was impressed with her, especially when she told her that her father was Oxford educated and that she hoped to own her own accountancy business one day, once she'd finished her university business degree, obviously.

'She seems like a very well-balanced, studious young lady – lovely darling, lovely,' Mums had said, by way of approval.

That weekend though, Jess was reluctantly visiting friends of her parents who lived in Sidcup. Apparently, they owned a luxury caravan they never stopped banging on about.

'Anyone would think it was a bloody Malibu Mansion and not a piece of tin on wheels with a chemical toilet,' she'd said, rolling her eyes. 'The only plus point about the whole weekend is the fact that their next door neighbour is Mr McFittie of McFittzville, so hopefully

I'll have something half-decent to look at while I lose the will to live.'

I'd finally told Jess about the possibility of my going along to watch JJ and his gang do some graffing. Jess had laughed when I'd said the word graffing, and I'd laughed too, because even I could tell the way I pronounced it sounded stupid.

'I knew it!' Jess had said excitedly. 'Tonight. Something's going to happen. I can feel it in my waters.'

'Don't be ridiculous,' I'd snapped back in good humour. 'I'm only going to watch him paint.' Secretly, though, I was quite excited by the thought myself.

Jess sighed deeply. 'Always the bridesmaid, never the bride, me. Oh, and remember to wear warm clothes if you're out graffing. You'll freeze your bazookas off otherwise and he'll not want a bazookaless bride, will he?'

Jess was right. I did need to wrap up warm. Our balmy late summer evenings had been replaced with a breezy autumnal chill. After hours of fruitless deliberation, I settled for a navy and white striped long-sleeved T-shirt which I teamed with a pair of jeans that were ripped and scuffed and a bit worn-looking. 'Distressed' the woman in the boutique had called them.

'I know *just* how they feel,' Mums had retorted as she counted out one hundred and fifty pounds in notes. I pulled on a cream beanie hat from Miss Sixty that Tave had given me last Christmas together with a matching scarf and I tried not to think about her as I stepped into my furry boots. A measly beanie hat was all I had left to show for all those years of friendship. I hadn't heard from Tave in ages, despite leaving numerous texts and voice messages. At first, I had tried to tell myself that she must be busy with school stuff and would get in touch eventually, but as the weeks had gone by, I had lost all hope of ever hearing from her again. I had to face facts: I was *persona non grata*. Now that I was out of sight, I was out of mind. So much for twelve years of friendship, huh? So what if our circumstances had changed, I was still *me*. Can you really throw away over a decade of being close with someone just because they don't live in a big house any more? I mean, how shallow is that?

I adjusted my beanie hat and tried to ignore the heaviness in my chest. Tave was now simply part of LBL (Life Before London), a life that had to be confined to the past if I had any hope of having a future. I checked myself in the mirror as I pulled on my chunky black cardigan coat and caught the look of sadness staring back at me. To combat it, I decided to pull as many silly faces as I could to try to make myself laugh. After the fifth attempt where I poked my tongue out, pushed my nose up into 'a piggy' and crossed my eyes, I managed a smile. Small steps, I told myself, small steps.

So there I was, making my way up towards the bus stop that takes you towards Ladbroke Grove when it suddenly struck. What *was* I thinking? It was never a firm arrangement that I would go and watch JJ and his friends 'do a piece'. He had only really invited me in passing. What if he was just being polite in the way that

people are so as not to hurt your feelings? I flashed the
bus driver my bus pass.

'Would you mind letting me know when we're
approaching the SmartSave car park?' I requested,
smiling at him politely.

'You what?' he barked, startling me. I had noticed that
there were not too many friendly bus drivers in London.

'Not to worry,' I stammered as I sat down.

I would have to try to be inconspicuous, suss out who
JJ was with before letting myself be seen by anyone. In
other words, I would hide. Cowardly, I know, but I had
been pretty brave already, all things considered,
venturing out on public transport – *alone* – to watch a
boy who might not even be that pleased to see me spray
graffiti on a wall.

'You,' the bus driver barked, startling me again.
'SmartSave car park, next stop.'

It felt like there was no going back.

# Chapter 10

I positioned myself behind a wall next to a stack of shopping trolleys and peered around the corner. I could just make out JJ, although it was difficult because it was already dark and he was dressed top to toe in black: black puffa coat, jeans and a hat; even his trainers were black. In fact, I wasn't even sure it was him.

There were four or five others with him, all sitting down by a wall covered in colourful aerosol shapes. I mentally planned my entrance. I would casually walk over as if I'd been shopping in SmartSave. Perhaps I would run in and grab a milkshake or something, make it look authentic. I'd say 'Oh hi,' as if I was surprised to see him. 'Yeah, right, I think I remember you saying something about coming down here to do some graffing.' No, no, not graffing. Jess had laughed when I'd said it earlier. It sounded stupid. 'To do some . . . some art, yeah. Just been shopping . . . yeah, why not, I'd love to hang out for a bit and watch . . .'

'Grace. Grace, is that you?' I spun round. Oh no. It was JJ. This was not supposed to happen. 'What are you doing hiding behind the wall?' he asked, perplexed.

'I'm not *hiding*,' I protested, quickly adding, 'I was just, um, trying to get a signal on my phone.' It was a feasible excuse and I felt pleased with myself.

'*Riiight,*' JJ said, clearly humouring me. 'I was hoping you'd come down,' he added.

'You were?' I replied, relieved. Perhaps it had not been a wasted journey after all.

'Yeah,' he said, smiling. 'Come on, I'll introduce you to the lads.' We walked towards the wall, him a few steps in front of me.

'Grace, this is Trucker, Ultimatum and Zone,' he said, introducing me to the three boys standing before me. I assumed those couldn't possibly be their real names. Zone gave me a big smile and nodded. The others just mumbled 'All right' under their breath. I noticed a couple of younger boys lurking around in the background. They were too far away to be introduced properly but JJ referred to them as the Dulcie twins from the estate. He looked at me a little apologetically.

'They're psyching themselves up,' he said, attempting to justify his friends' lack of interest in me. 'They don't like distractions before doing a piece.'

'Oh, sorry,' I said hastily. 'Should I go?'

'Don't be daft.' JJ shook his head. 'Besides, who else is going to light my ciggies and hold my spray paint for me?' I hoped he was joking.

'What you been up to this week?' he asked, absent-mindedly checking the nozzle on one of his spray cans. 'Staying out of trouble I hope.'

I giggled. It sounded girly. 'Not much,' I shrugged. It wasn't a lie. 'My English teacher has asked me to audition for a part in *Othello* – the school play – and I think my mother might be about to embark on an affair with the

Russian next door.' I knew she wasn't really about to have an affair with Boris – he'd only ever been round to our house twice, once to fix the boiler and the next when he was forced to eat one of Mums's pies – but it made my week sound far more exciting than it really was, so I said it anyway.

'Just the usual, then?' JJ smiled, the corners of his cupid bow lips curling upwards. He hadn't shaved again and the stubble on his chin looked like it might be a little scratchy. 'That's cool about the school play though. What's *Othello* about anyway? Is it a comedy?'

I nudged him playfully. 'Silly,' I said.

'What?' He shrugged, deadpan.

'You've really never heard of *Othello*?' I asked.

He began kicking invisible objects as he looked down at the floor. 'No,' he said quietly, 'I haven't.'

I had made him feel bad. Worse, I had made him feel stupid.

'It's classic Shakespeare,' I said, my tone less incredulous. 'It's more of a tragedy than a comedy, although he did write comedies too.' I was hoping to make him feel a little better. 'Anyway, surely you've heard of *Hamlet*? I mean, it's probably Shakespeare's most famous work and it's the name of your estate and everything.'

'Never really thought about it,' JJ said, still unable to make eye contact with me.

Oh God, he really hadn't heard of *Hamlet* either!

'You see,' JJ said, his face a little flushed, 'I'm as thick as a brick and you're dead clever.'

'Noooo,' I said, wishing I'd never said anything about

the stupid play now. 'Don't think that. Who cares anyway? Have you ever needed to know about *Othello* or *Hamlet* before? It's not as if anyone has ever asked you to quote a line from Shakespeare in a job interview, is it?' I said.

'Nope, can't say that they have,' he agreed.

'Well there you are then,' I shrugged, smiling.

'But then again, I haven't really been to any job interviews. Not proper ones, like in an office and that.'

'Oh,' I said.

'So why do they teach Shakespeare in school if no one really needs to know about it? I mean, if it don't help you get a job and that?' JJ asked. It was a good question.

'I'm not entirely sure myself,' I said, and we both began to laugh, which helped to disperse the moment of awkwardness.

'Will your mum give you a hard time about taking time off your studies to rehearse?' he asked. 'Or is she, er, too busy with the Russian?'

I felt a pang of guilt about saying that Mums was having an affair. It made her sound a little tacky.

'She's fine about it; she thinks it's good I've got some extra-curricular activities to keep me amused,' I said. 'She's not too keen about the fact that it's being held at Hamlet youth centre though. She doesn't really want me hanging around up there.' I felt compelled to be honest with him. I figured if he knew the truth, albeit diluted, I wouldn't have to explain why I was hiding our friendship from her. 'She's a bit of a snob,' I smiled, hoping he would understand. 'What can I say?'

JJ smiled. 'Well, I guess it's only to be expected. If

you've lived most of your life like a member of the royal family then I can only imagine what she thinks of our estate – and the people living in it. It's a shame she can't see past the stereotypes, though. It's not exactly plush but there are some cool people living there from all walks of life. It's not all doleheads and drop-outs. Take my mate Zone over there,' he said, pointing to him. 'I've known him since we were three years old. He's one of the most talented street painters in the world. We're hoping to go to Amsterdam and the US together someday. Spraying is much more respected as an art form there than it is here. He's my best mate,' JJ said, 'I'd do anything for him.'

I smiled back, touched by his affection towards his friend. 'What's his real name?' I asked out of nosiness.

'Sid.' JJ laughed a little. 'Sid Sims.'

'Oh,' I said. I think I'd have stuck with Zone too.

'And there's other interesting people who live on Hamlet too, like Mr Dent at number ninety-three. He won the Victoria Cross in the war, and his wife was killed by a bomb on Bridge Street during the Blitz. He still talks about her,' JJ said a little sadly. 'And Mrs Jacobs at number fifty-six – she's a white witch who reads palms and tarot cards. She predicted that a tornado would hit America in the 1950s, got her name in the papers and everything. She showed me the cuttings once.'

'Wow!' I said, impressed. I'd never met a real witch before.

'Cal, my brother, would love to hear all about Mr Dent,' I said. 'He's obsessed with war and anything to do with it.'

'Maybe we'll take him up to meet him then,' JJ said.

'Mr Dent's a bit unsteady on his legs now, so I get him the occasional bag of shopping, you know, because he can't get about so well.'

'That's lovely of you,' I said softly. He quickly looked away, embarrassed.

'So you see all sorts of people live on Hamlet. It's sad that people have all these conceptions.'

'You mean *pre*conceptions,' I said, 'and misconceptions.'

'Yeah, and any other kind of 'ceptions you can think of,' he said. I think I had unintentionally embarrassed him again because he quickly added, 'Like I said, I know I'm a bit thick and that I don't talk properly, but I know what I mean and I mean what I know, if you know what I mean.' He raised an eyebrow.

'I think so,' I replied, smiling.

'And I know that this is what I want to do,' he said, holding up his spray can and pretending to squirt it in my face. I squealed and stepped back. 'This,' he said, looking at the spray can and giving it a little shake which made a rather pleasing rattling sound, 'is my ticket to fame and fortune.'

'Go forth and spray your way to success!' I said, theatrically. He smiled at me brightly and I smiled back, and for a fraction of a second I thought he was about to do something ridiculous like kiss me, but instead he saluted me as if I were an officer in the army giving him a command.

For the next twenty minutes, I watched in complete awe

as JJ and his mates set about spraying the wall in front of me. JJ did most of the outline as well as a lot of the detail. He was clearly the most talented out of the five, despite his modesty. It took me a while to fathom what it was they were actually painting. After a time, it began to take the shape of a sort of mystical creature, like a dinosaur with wings.

'So is it a dinosaur or a dragon?' I asked as he stood next to me, taking a few moments' break to view his work in progress. 'Whichever, it's very good.'

'Hmmm,' he said, putting his finger up to his mouth thoughtfully. 'It's not a dinosaur, but then again I don't think it's a dragon either.' He paused for a moment. 'I think it's a dragosaurus.' He glanced at me and laughed.

I laughed too. 'One dinosaur plus one dragon equals a dragosaurus, yes, of course,' I said, feeling happier than I had in ages.

'It's not even halfway finished yet though,' he said. 'He's going to be breathing fire and the fire is going to spell out the words *Fu Man Crew*, which is the name of our crew, obviously,' he explained. 'I think we should make him yellow but Zone is on the money for green. What do you reckon?'

'Me?' I said, a little surprised he had asked my opinion on what was clearly a very important decision. 'Well, er, green seems a little obvious, I guess, and so does yellow, well, I suppose. Personally though, I'd make him purple,' I said, 'because I think that's what colour a dragosaurus should be.'

I looked up at him and noticed he was staring at me

intently. It made me feel uncomfortable yet oddly excited. 'You know something?' he said softly, throwing his roll-up to the floor and squashing it with his foot. 'You are absolutely right.' Then he pulled the top of my beanie hat right over my face and ran off back to his crew before I could protest.

I suppose I felt a bit silly, just standing there in the dark, propped up against the wall of SmartSave car park on my own, watching him paint. I was mesmerised by the way he worked with the aerosol cans as if they were paintbrushes and the wall a canvas. This wasn't the sort of art I was used to seeing hanging on the walls of Embers or in my father's shop, but the precision of his movements and the concentration etched on his face, which was slightly rosy with the October night air, were strangely thrilling to watch.

I rubbed my gloved hands together tightly and wrapped my arms round my chest as I moved from foot to foot to keep warm.

'You're cold,' he said, putting his can of paint down.

'A little,' I admitted, wishing I'd taken proper heed of Jess's advice. I really was beginning to freeze my bazookas off, just as she had warned.

'We're almost done,' he said. 'If you like, you can come back to mine and have some sausage and mash for tea. My ma won't mind.' He looked at me expectantly. The truth was that I really wanted to say 'Yes! I'd love that,' but I was anxious about meeting his family – I mean, holy craparama, I'd not known him that long! Worse, I was even more nervous about Mums's reaction if she knew I'd been mixing with people from *that* estate again, let alone dining with them. It would've been exceptionally impolite to say no, though, and he might never ask me again if I did. I quickly sent Mums a text saying I was having dinner at Jess's house and she replied saying, *OK Darling. Have fun!* So, with that sorted, I nodded and said to JJ, 'Sausage and mash sounds wonderful.'

# Chapter 11

'You'll have to excuse the flat,' JJ said as we made our way up in the stinky lift. 'It's not dirty or anything; it's just that when seven people live together in a small place it gets a bit, er, cramped.'

'Are you sure it's OK if I come up?' I asked, sensing he was already trying to justify what might lie ahead.

'Course. You made the effort to brave the cold and come and watch me paint, a bit of dinner is the least I can offer you for your troubles. If you don't mind eating with the lower classes, that is,' he said, teasing me.

I shot him a 'Don't be so silly' look, even though I was a little nervous of what to expect.

'Just to warn you,' he said, 'my ma likes to chat. She'll probably ask you loads of questions. Feel free not to answer. And the kids,' he rolled his eyes, 'they will just want to climb all over you, so don't feel bad about telling them to shove off or anything. And like I said, the flat's hardly Buckingham Palace, it's not like what you're used to . . .'

I smiled. '*Was* used to,' I said.

He smiled back and there was that dimple again.

'Eh, you're back. Come in, come in. Shut that door. You're bringing in the draught, so you is. And who is this fine lady? You didn't say about bringing back a guest for your tea, Jay.' Mrs Jones attempted to look at her son crossly but failed. 'I would've got the good plates out, so I would.' JJ's mum couldn't have stood more than five foot tall yet her formidable presence and strong Northern Irish accent filled the room. She gripped me by the hand and looked me up and down. 'Got the Irish in you, so I see.' She pointed to my auburn hair and smiled approvingly.

'It's very nice to meet you Mrs Jones,' I smiled politely. 'I must apologise for not bringing you flowers or anything but it was all a bit, well, impromptu.' I looked at JJ nervously.

'Flowers my arse,' she said, waving her hands in a shooing gesture. 'Mary. The name's Mary. Ma if you prefer.' She grabbed hold of me with both arms and pulled me in close to her chest for a hug. 'Doesn't she sound adorable, JJ? The voice, like off the telly?' She smelled faintly of gin. 'I do wish you'd said you were bringing someone special back, Jay,' she chastised him again. 'It's only sausage and colcannon tonight.'

'Really, that's fine,' I said quickly, embarrassed that she thought I was special and deserved something fancy. I wondered what on earth colcannon was and if I would like it, but I figured it couldn't be any worse than Mums's cooking.

'Where are the twins and Mickey and Joe? Is Marianne in?' JJ asked as he took off his coat and helped me out of mine.

'Marianne's bathing the twins and Joe and Mickey are

playing on that game thing you got them. Haven't torn themselves away from it all night, so they haven't,' Mrs Jones said, wiping her small, weather-beaten hands on the tabard she was wearing. 'Make yourself at home, Grace. Move that muck from the nice chair, JJ, and let the lady take a seat.'

I glanced around the small living room. Myriad picture frames containing photographs of smiley-faced children enjoying family Christmases and black and white pictures of couples dressed in old-fashioned clothes hung on the fading wallpaper. Comics and women's weekly magazines were randomly scattered across the small coffee table and a large green sofa which had the perfect imprint of an iron burnt on to one of its threadbare seats. A small fire with fake plastic logs glowed in the corner and collections of well-worn, mud-splattered children's shoes were neatly lined against one wall. Everything looked so worn and old and faded, like a sepia photograph. I wondered if it had ever been new in the first place.

'Can I offer you a nice brew, Grace?' Mrs Jones called from the kitchen where JJ was helping her. 'I think we might even have some Earl Grey left over from when Father Philips baptised the twins.'

'Ordinary tea will be absolutely fine,' I called back uncomfortably. 'Thanks very much.'

Two identical little girls walked into the living room dressed in matching pink pyjamas, their dark hair freshly washed and wavy. An older girl with long dark hair, who I guessed was probably a bit younger than me, closely followed them. She had to be Marianne.

'Hi,' she said, smiling at me as she moved some comics on to the small glass coffee table. 'I tell you, trying to get them out of that bath is a total nightmare.' She rolled her eyes. 'They're such water babies.' She glanced lovingly at her little twin sisters as they plonked themselves down in front of the small TV. 'Say hello, girls,' Marianne said, sounding far more grown-up than she looked. The twins turned their heads towards me.

'Hiya!' they said in eerie unison.

'Hi,' I replied brightly. 'I'm Grace.'

'Are you JJ's girlfriend?' one of them asked. I felt myself turn crimson.

Marianne laughed.

'You're very pretty,' the other twin said.

'Thank you,' I smiled, 'And so are you. Both of you.'

'I'm Marianne,' JJ's sister said, giving me a friendly hug. 'JJ's not stopped talking about you since he met you,' she whispered. 'Although he'd kill me if he heard me telling you that.'

I smiled back coyly as a wave of excitement washed over me. Had he really been talking about me?

'Come and get your supper, girls,' JJ's mum called from in the kitchen. 'I'm just about to dish up. Where are Mickey and Joe?'

'Mickey, Joe!' JJ shouted from the kitchen. 'Drop the game and get your butts out here now, guys – grubs up!'

'Can I help with anything?' I asked, feeling awkward with everyone rushing around me.

'Don't be ridiculous,' Mrs Jones said. 'You're our guest, so you are.'

I noticed JJ was extending a small half-moon-shaped dining table into its full capacity and I watched him as he struggled, unsure whether to ask if he needed some help.

'C'mon kids, we're sitting at the table tonight. We've got company,' Mrs Jones said, putting placemats next to the mismatching cutlery.

'We'll have to get the spare chair out of the cupboard, Jay, you know, one of the fold-up ones we use at Christmas.'

'Really, please don't on my account,' I said, panicking at the trouble she was going to.

We sat around the small wooden table, eight of us. The two boys had made a late entrance and nodded at me, smiling. I noticed that the older boy had a similar dimple to JJ's, except his was on the opposite cheek.

'This is Grace,' Mrs Jones said, 'she's a friend of Jay's.' Then she introduced me to all of her children in order of age. There was JJ, seventeen of course, then Marianne who seemed surprisingly old for her thirteen years, Joe (the one with the dimple) twelve, Mickey ten, and the twins Ria and Sinead who had recently turned six.

'And me,' said Mrs Jones, 'I'm a hundred and five!' She laughed heartily.

I smiled and said, 'Oh no, no.' I figured she couldn't possibly be much older than Mums, especially since she had six-year-old twins, but her friendly face looked quite lined and worn out. I wondered if perhaps that's what comes of having a hard life.

JJ looked at me from across the table and smiled. I started to feel a little more relaxed.

'Dig in,' Mrs Jones said. 'Anyone for brown sauce?'

I felt self-conscious as I cut into my sausage and wished I had a napkin to hide behind.

'Do you live in a castle?' one of the twins asked, pouring ketchup all over her mountain of mashed potato. 'JJ said you are a princess who lives in a castle with horses and a swimming pool and servants and that.'

JJ elbowed his little sister playfully in the ribs. 'No I didn't, Ria!' he said, clearly embarrassed.

'You talk like how the Queen does,' Sinead added.

Mickey started to giggle.

'That's enough, girls,' Mrs Jones shot the twins a stern look. 'JJ tells us you've recently moved to the area, Grace.'

'Yes,' I said, trying not to think too much about the colourful lumps in my mashed potato and what they might actually be. 'Erwine Street, just off Goldborne Road.'

'Know it well,' she smiled, displaying a small piece of cabbage lodged between her teeth.

'JJ tells me you're in the Sixth Form at Kinsmead. Are you planning on going to university?'

'I hope to,' I smiled. 'It depends on my grades, but my parents, well, they're really hoping I make it to Oxford or Cambridge.'

Mrs Jones nodded with interest. 'JJ says you want to be an actress.'

I glanced at JJ who mouthed the word 'sorry' to me.

'Well, I tell you, you've got the face and the looks for it, so you have,' Mrs Jones said. 'There's something of an old-time quality about her, don't you think Jay?'

JJ smiled. 'I think she'd make a good actress – she's a

right drama queen!' he laughed

'Hey!' I said, mock-indignantly, and we all started laughing.

Mickey let out a loud burp.

'Mickey!' Mrs Jones shrieked, 'Mind your manners, there are ladies present, so there are.' Mrs Jones gave her son a gentle flick around the ear.

''Tis a cheeky one, this one,' she said. 'Ah well, I suppose it's better out than in, son.'

JJ looked slightly sheepish and I smiled at him reassuringly.

'Have you seen any of JJ's work, Grace?' Mrs Jones asked. She had spooned up the last of her dinner even though I wasn't even halfway through mine. 'Aye, he's a talented boy, this one.' She ruffled JJ's hair. JJ rolled his eyes, embarrassed.

'Don't go there, Ma,' he said.

'He doesn't like to brag,' Mrs Jones said, 'so I do it for him, so I do. Don't know where he gets it from – the artistic stuff. I have trouble drawing breath!' She began laughing heartily again and it sounded like a hundred pots and pans crashing to the floor.

Sinead was making a happy face out of her potato, sausage and peas.

She looked up at me. 'Does your daddy live in a prison?' she asked innocently. The room fell awkwardly silent for a moment and I felt JJ's mum gently kick her daughter under the table. Everyone stared down into their plates not sure what to say or whether they should look at each other.

'Sinead,' Mrs Jones said, glaring at her daughter, 'hush your mouth!' Everyone shifted in their seats. 'I'm terribly sorry, Grace, she has a vivid imagination does this one.'

I glanced at JJ, who looked mortified, then turned and smiled at Sinead, who was looking up at me, non-plussed. 'Yes,' I whispered loudly enough for everyone to hear, 'he does.' Sinead clapped her hands together and let out a squeal of excitement. I couldn't help myself – I started to laugh. Then Sinead laughed, and one by one everybody joined in until we were all laughing together.

After dessert – a frozen cake-thing with ice cream in the middle, which I learned is called arctic roll – I agreed to read the twins a story before bedtime. I snuggled between them in bed in the small room they shared with Marianne and her impressive collection of True East boy-band posters.

'Do you think you will marry JJ?' Ria asked me once I'd finished the story for the second time. I was aware that JJ was now standing in the doorway listening and I didn't say anything because I was too busy trying not to blush. Instead I laughed a little nervously, kissed her on the forehead, and did the same with Sinead before I left the tiny room.

'You were amazing with the twins,' JJ said as we walked through the pardon towards my home. 'They really loved you.'

'Thanks,' I said, feeling surprisingly warm despite the cold night air. 'Your family are so lovely and welcoming,'

I added. 'And the twins are adorable.'

'They come out with some hilarious things,' JJ said. I thought he must have been referring to Ria's comment about me and JJ getting married. 'I mean, truly absurd.'

'Is it?' I asked, finding myself feeling slightly irked that he would think being married to me absurd. We both looked at each other very quickly and then looked away again.

'Well, as if someone like you would ever marry someone like me,' JJ said, laughing. 'I mean, you come from a good background and know about fine art, Shakespeare, and all that stuff. You've lived in a huge house with swimming pools and you've been to posh schools and operas and travelled around the world. Whereas me, well, I'm just a council estate boy. I don't know nothing, apart from how to graff, and the furthest I've ever travelled is Southend-on-Sea.'

I stopped walking for a second and turned to look at JJ. 'You know if I said something like that you'd call me a snob!' I said, a little crushed.

'So would you marry me, then?' JJ said, slipping me a sneaky sideways glance and quickly adding, 'Not that I'm asking you to, you understand. I know you've met my family and everything, but we haven't even kissed yet!'

My heart began to beat a little faster.

'No, but you and Janice Brady have,' I blurted out. It was exactly the sort of thing I'd promised myself I wouldn't say because it sounded as though I might actually be bothered.

'Whoa!' JJ said, taking a step back. 'Where did *that* come from?'

I shrugged. 'Oh, it was just something Jess told me.'

'Jessica Beaks?' JJ asked. 'Old Beaksy!'

'Hey, I said, 'she's my friend!'

JJ laughed. 'Beaksy's OK. Loves a gossip though.'

I couldn't disagree with him there.

'Not sure where she got that bit of info from,' he said, 'but it's way off the mark.'

'Really?' I said, sounding a little more pleased than I wanted to.

'I heard Janice had a bit of a crush on me once,' JJ said, looking down shyly. 'But I don't know if it was true and it certainly wasn't recip . . . recipro . . . I certainly never fancied her back or nothing.'

My heart began spinning like a catherine wheel inside my chest.

'She's not my type for one thing.'

'No?' I said, intrigued as to who might be. 'Why's that?'

'I like girls to be more like, well girls, I suppose. I'm not into those loud types who're all brash and in your face and stuff. I like feminine girls, you know, someone a bit softer, a bit more . . . what's the word I'm looking for?' JJ paused and frowned as he thought.

'Refined?' I suggested.

'That's it, refined!' he said. 'I like girls who're refined and polite and who don't burp and fart in public . . . '

I stared at JJ in horror. He *knew* girls who burped and farted in public?

'Kind girls, the sort you wouldn't mind taking home to meet your mum.' He nudged me gently. 'A girl like you.'

Someone get me a glass of water!

'Oh yeah,' I said, not sure whether to believe him. 'Really?'

'Yeah,' he said, meeting my gaze, 'really.'

We both laughed a little awkwardly for a moment, unsure where next to take the conversation. As we walked, I found myself wanting to ask JJ about his father. He had never mentioned him.

'So,' I said, wondering how best to broach the subject and settling for subtle as a brick, 'your dad . . .'

'What about him?' JJ didn't seem at all surprised by my bringing him up.

'Do you see him?' I asked. 'It's just that you've never mentioned him . . .'

JJ smiled wistfully. 'No. I don't see him.'

'Oh,' I said. 'I'm sorry.'

'He died of a heart attack just after the twins were born. He was only forty-four.'

I put my hand up to my mouth involuntarily. 'Oh JJ, I'm really so sorry.'

JJ stuffed his hands in his pockets and stared at the pavement. 'Don't be,' he said. 'It sounds harsh, but I reckon we're better off without him. He was no good really; in and out of prison most of his adult life. So you see, we have more in common than you think.' I looked at him, his face calm and expressionless, only his eyes betrayed him. They flickered with sadness and regret. I reached out and squeezed his hand reassuringly, which was an unusually touchy-feely thing for me to do. He squeezed back, which made my legs feel a bit wobbly.

'I vowed to my ma that I'd never end up like him,' JJ said with conviction, 'which is why she was so upset when I got in trouble with the police for spraying. I promised I would make it up to her, stay out of trouble, keep my nose clean, anything not to go down the same route as my dad.' He looked down at the pavement. 'One day, I'll make enough money to get us all out of this dump,' he said, glancing back in the direction of Hamlet Tower. 'I mean, I know it's my home and everything, but would you really want to bring your kids up there if you had the choice? I want to be able to make a better life for us all. One where we don't have to struggle, and Ma doesn't have to hold down three jobs. I want to be able to buy the kids decent toys for Christmas and not second-hand stuff from charity shops. Do you know where I'm coming from?'

I nodded, even though I didn't, not really.

'I'm sorry,' he said, 'I'm supposed to be cheering you up. Not doing such a good job, eh?' He smiled.

But he *was* cheering me up, despite his sad tales of life on Hamlet estate and his dad and everything. It felt so unbelievably good to talk, just to walk and talk so naturally. I'd never met a boy I could talk to so easily. I didn't have to think too hard about what I was saying or whether I was being clever or funny enough. Not that I didn't want to impress him. I just wasn't as self-conscious as I had been with other boys.

I blinked at JJ and wondered how someone like him

could be so very different from how I imagined he would be. He was so much more emotionally intelligent than the boys I had known, a quality I realised that five thousand pounds a term could never buy you. If only Mums could have put her prejudices to one side and met him, she would have seen that he was nothing like the stereotype she had built up in her mind from newspapers and crime documentaries.

We stood a little way outside the red door to 146 Erwine Street. I still couldn't quite bring myself to call it home.

'Well,' I said, a little awkwardly, 'thanks for inviting me to dinner. I'll have to return the favour sometime.' Suddenly I didn't care about what Mums might say if I did.

'And thank *you* for coming to watch me paint,' he replied, holding my hand up and swinging it in his. We were both shuffling on the spot a little in the darkness, the haziness of the street lamps giving our faces an orangey glow. It was cold and I watched as the condensation of my breath in the air intertwined with his. 'I really hoped you would,' he added.

'I need all the friends I can get round here,' I said, trying to lighten the sudden intensity that had come from nowhere and lodged itself between us.

'You can never have too many friends,' agreed JJ. He let go of my hand and began to play with the scarf around my neck, first unwrapping it and then wrapping it up again.

I could feel my heart begin to pound underneath my

coat and my ears begin to burn as the blood rushed furiously around my body. Oh God, was Jess right? Were we going to kiss? He smiled at me and I noticed we were much closer together now.

'I'd better go,' I stammered, holding my ground as I felt the gentle tug of the scarf around the back of my neck. 'Mums gets terribly stressy when it's dark and I'm not back by ten – sad, I realise, but I'm sure she still thinks I'm Cal's age and –'

He nodded and pulled my beanie hat over my face again.

'Hey!' I said from beneath my woollen mask. As he rolled it up he was kissing me. His hot, wet mouth pressed against mine with an urgency I'd never experienced in previous kisses. I felt myself go weak in his arms and he caught me, supporting my weight as he held my face in his warm, soft hands. I closed my eyes and let myself go right along with it, swept away by his tenderness and warmth. The tip of his nose was cold as it brushed against mine and he tasted of fresh mint, as if he had taken care not to smell of cigarettes. His floppy hair tickled my forehead as he stopped for breath and he gently brushed his lips against mine, showering them with short soft kisses that made me feel as warm as hot buttered toast from the outside in. In that moment, I forgot everything I had ever worried about: school, home, Mums and Oxshott, even Dad. When we finally stopped kissing, I felt like I had come through a different time zone. Like life had just begun all over again.

'Do you kiss all your friends like that?' he smiled,

breathing into the cold night as he held me in his arms, his puffa jacket making a funny scrunching sound as it rubbed against my faux fur coat.

'Do *you*?' I shot back.

'Only ones who don't know what arctic roll is,' he said smiling, the warmth of his breath gently tickling the small part of my exposed neck.

'It tastes lovely,' I said, 'arctic roll.'

'So do you,' he said. His lips were velvety soft, but his stubble was beginning to scratch my chin. I giggled.

'I've wanted to do that since the moment I met you,' he said, more seriously this time. 'I was hoping it might be like the frog prince: you'd kiss me and I'd turn into something great.'

I wanted to say, 'You're already great,' but I was too spellbound to speak. I desperately didn't want to let him go but I knew Mums could look out of the window at any given second. 'I really must go,' I said, more urgently this time. 'It's getting rather late.'

'Yes, it is, *rather*,' he said, but there was no sarcasm in his mimicry, just a strange sort of affection that made me feel quite light-headed.

'Hope to see you soon,' he said, 'maybe next week?'

I wasn't sure if I could wait that long before I saw him again, but I knew it would be difficult, what with school and study and Mums guarding me like the Crown Jewels.

'Perhaps you'll come and watch me paint again?'

'I might just do that,' I smiled, trying to play it cool, when really I felt like bursting into song like Maria in *The Sound of Music*.

'Wear your thermals next time though, eh?' He smiled and kissed my hand as he walked off into the dark. I tried to think of something funny to say back, but I wasn't quick enough and when I'd turned round he'd gone, just like that.

In my boxroom bedroom I sat by the window and looked out into the inky darkness. The tiny lights coming from Hamlet Tower glinted and twinkled in the distance. For once it almost looked quite pretty, like a giant Christmas tree covered in fairy lights.

Like a blanket to keep me warm, I wrapped myself up in the memory of the evening: the dragosaurus and JJ's family. They had seemed such a loving, close-knit unit. It made me feel a little sad about my own family and how, although I knew we loved each other, we clammed up like oysters when it came to voicing our true feelings.

I lay back on my bed and wrapped my duvet around me; I felt the need to hold on to something. Thoughts spun round my head so fast, I began to feel a little dizzy. How strange life is. If someone had told me six months ago that I would be living in a run-down part of London and that I would meet the most amazing, kind, talented and gorgeous boy from a council estate and we would end up kissing, I would have laughed myself into a coma.

Horrid niggling thoughts also crept in. Mums. I'd be collecting my pension before she'd allow me out again if she got wind I was involved with a boy from *that* estate, let alone *kissing* him. And I wondered what would possibly come of this? After all, aside from our fathers' respective felonies, we had very little in common. But who needs doubts? Doubts are for, well, doubters. For now, I just wanted to bask in the rosy glow of our kiss. This being poor business, it wasn't half as bad as I had first thought. I sighed happily as I clicked my light switch on and off, on and off, on and off. Seconds later, I felt sure I saw a tiny light high up in Hamlet Tower do exactly the same thing.

# Chapter 12

JJ stayed true to his word. He texted me on Sunday to say that he'd arranged for Cal and me to visit Mr Dent at number ninety-three the next day after school. I made Cal swear on his original German army helmet that he wouldn't tell Mums and he was so excited about meeting a real live war veteran that he readily agreed.

Waiting for JJ by the entrance to Sometime Place, I had dancing butterflies in my stomach and my mouth felt dry. It was the first time we'd seen each other since 'the kiss' and I wasn't quite sure how to act.

Be yourself, I told myself, but suddenly that was easier said than done. My arms felt awkward hanging down by my sides and I had clean forgotten how to stand comfortably and kept shuffling from foot to foot. Would we kiss again? The thought sent a small shiver down my spine, but there was fat chance of anything like that happening with Cal fidgeting by my side. Besides, I didn't even know if JJ would want to, though I hoped that, like me, he would.

'Hiya,' JJ said, smiling, as he strolled up. He looked more gorgeous than ever in his baggy skate pants, with his long, floppy fringe hanging in his eyes – a vision of pure, dishevelled sexiness. He leaned forward and kissed me on the cheek. I closed my eyes and bit my lip.

'Glad you could make it,' he said softly, then turned to Cal with a grin. 'Hi, I'm JJ. You must be Cal.'

Mr Dent's tiny flat looked like a museum. Everything about it was old: the furniture, the wallpaper, the fading flowery curtains. JJ and I stood together, staring up at a wall of black and white photographs. There were many of a young woman with a soft, rounded face and porcelain skin. She had a warm, friendly smile and sparkling eyes. Her hair was curled up at the front on both sides. I'd seen similar hairstyles in old photographs that Mums had shown me of Auntie Betsy and my dad's mother, Grandma Phoebe, who died when I was small.

'Ahh, there she is, my beautiful gel,' old Mr Dent said, his watery eyes coming to life as he looked up at the photographs. 'Ain't she a beauty?'

'Yes, she is lovely,' I said, suddenly feeling a little choked up. JJ gave my hand a little squeeze, as if detecting my sudden wave of emotion.

'It should have been the other way round you know,' said Mr Dent, his voice wobbling.

'Come on now, Mr Dent,' JJ said soothingly, 'you know you'll only upset yourself.'

'I should've been the one to go, not her,' the old man continued, ignoring JJ and reaching for a picture with a shaking hand. 'Look at this one,' he said, taking it from the wall. 'Don't we look like a couple of carrots half-scraped in that, eh love?'

I had absolutely no idea what he meant. I figured it had to be an old war term or something, so I just nodded and said, 'You make a wonderful couple.'

Mr Dent didn't move his eyes from the picture. 'I still miss her like it was yesterday. Think of her every day, I do. She was a wonderful lady. A brilliant wife. She would've made the best mother in the world. Bloody Jerries.'

I swallowed hard.

'There never was another for me you know,' he continued. 'She was it. My one true love. I could never love another after I lost her.'

'I'm so sorry,' I managed to say, even though it physically hurt to speak now that the lump in my throat had got so big.

'It never leaves you, you know, true love. It stays here,' he said, banging his fist against his chest, 'right here till the day you die. God bless you, Maud darling.' He kissed the picture, placed it back on the wall and turned round to look at Cal, who was rifling through an old wooden box marked *War Memories*.

'Right then, lad,' he said as he composed himself, 'if it's stories you're after . . . Put the pot on, JJ, and get your good lady friend a seat. I don't know, no manners, these young men of today,' he winked at me as JJ turned and made his way towards the kitchen, 'wouldn't know what treating a lady meant if it was spelled out to them in six-foot-high letters!'

The following morning Cal burst into my boxroom bedroom without so much as a knock. 'Grace,' he whispered loudly, 'are you asleep?'

'Yes,' I groaned, pulling my duvet over my head. 'Go away.'

I felt him sit down on the edge of my bed. Reluctantly I rolled over on to my back and peered over the edge of the duvet. He was already dressed for school.

'You're keen,' I said huskily. 'Are you really enjoying school *that* much?'

Cal shrugged.

'Is everything OK?' Cal didn't often come into my bedroom any more, not since he'd turned twelve. I sensed he wanted to talk. 'So, are you enjoying life at Kinsmead Comp?' I asked, rubbing my bleary eyes.

He shrugged again. 'I suppose.' Now I was worried.

'The other boys, the boys in your class . . . how are you getting on with them?'

'They're OK.'

I gave him a sideways glance. 'Hmmm, are you sure?'

'They weren't very friendly at first,' Cal admitted, 'called me names and stuff.'

'And stuff?'

'Oh you know, stole my bag and played football with it, pinned me up against the wall and kneed me in the goolies . . . the usual.'

'Oh Cal, why didn't you say anything?' I reached for his hand but he quickly folded his arms. 'I could've done something to help.'

'No need.' He blinked at me. 'I told them about Dad.'

'You did what?'

'I told them that Dad was in prison but that he had connections on the outside and was keeping an eye on things.' He winked conspiratorially.

'What did you say he was inside for?'

'Armed robbery.'

'Cal!'

'Well, it worked,' he said, defiantly. 'They haven't touched me since! Some of them are even sad enough to think that it's cool having a father in prison. They think it's some kind of accolade, being the son of a gangster.'

'You shouldn't tell such lies,' I said, trying to be cross with him and failing.

'Self-preservation, sis,' he said, patting the side of his nose with his finger. 'Self-preservation.'

'So everything's OK now, yes?'

'Yes. In fact, I almost quite like it there now. My history teacher, Mr Henry, is rather nice. He knows some impressive facts about World War II and has promised to bring in some family photos of his relatives who fought in it for me to have a look at,' he said, eyes wide with excitement.

'Great,' I replied, attempting to muster up some enthusiasm.

'Not that they would be as great as Mr Dent's collection. I mean, he was actually there, in the flesh. Nothing can beat that.' He paused. 'Did you know that the term "no man's land" derives from The Great War, otherwise known as World War I?'

I groaned again and turned away from him. It was far too early for war-talk.

'Oh, and by the way,' Cal said with a glint in his eyes, 'I just thought you might like to know – there's a huge picture of Piccalilli on the wall outside. Check it out. See you later, Graceless.'

'Cal! What did you say?' I called out to him, confused, but he'd scarpered. I sat up in bed abruptly. A picture of Piccalilli? What *was* he talking about? I padded over to the window and drew back the curtains. There, on the wall on the far side of the railway track, was a giant, spectacular picture of a beautiful dapple-grey horse. It looked as though it was galloping in the wind, its impressive mane and tail swishing behind it dramatically, nostrils flaring and black eyes shining brightly. Above it in big black letters were the words *Piccalilli Rides Again*, accompanied by a little dove that looked like it was flying alongside the horse, *my* horse. I rubbed my eyes, just to check I wasn't still dreaming. Oh my God! JJ, he must have painted Piccalilli for me! I stared at the image for ages, drinking in every detail. It must have taken him forever to paint. He would have had to climb over the wall during the night and work by flashlight – in the dark, in the cold! This was just the most romantic thing ever! I pressed my face against the window.

'Piccalilli . . . my beautiful Piccalilli,' I said under my breath, and then I realised tears were running down my cheeks and that I was going to be late for school.

As soon as Jess saw my face, she began screaming with delight. 'Oh my God you have *so* kissed, haven't you? I can tell!'

I nodded and squealed, unable to stop myself from joining in with her euphoria. Jess had been off school on Monday with a tummy bug, so this was the first time I'd seen her since Friday.

'This is just *immense*,' she said, eyes bulging beneath her glasses. She was almost speechless. *Almost.* 'What did I tell you? The Beakster is never wrong.' She puffed her chest out proudly.

I told her about Piccalilli.

'He spent all night spraying you a piece? Of your horse? On the railway wall? And he invited you to meet his family!' She was staring at me in excited disbelief. 'Holy crapoly! If I didn't like you so much I would hate you! No one's ever done anything even half as remotely romantic for me, you jammy old moo!' She gave me a playful shove.

I couldn't help smiling. Jess had been like a saviour to me since I'd moved to London. We had become close quickly – unusual for me, as it often takes me a while to open up and be myself with people. It was easy with Jess though. She was laid back and cool and, even though she was an incurable gossip and could be as subtle as a steam train, I knew that inside she had a heart of pure gold. I suddenly felt very lucky to have met her.

'This calls for a celebration!' she announced. 'Curly Wurlies and cappucinos on me! I want to know everything, in chronological order and in microscopic detail – no skipping bits,' she warned, dragging me off to the school café with a pace to rival an Olympic sprinter.

By Thursday, I still hadn't managed to see JJ and thank him for the picture of Piccalilli. It was all Mums's fault. She had flatly refused to allow me to set foot outside the front door because I had so much studying to do. I could hardly throw myself at her mercy and beg her to let me out to see him. I had good reason to believe that, had she known of my rendezvous with JJ, she would have bought a padlock for my boxroom bedroom door and locked me in. Still, Mums couldn't keep me a prisoner in my own home forever. I had an audition to go to, and nothing but nothing was going to stop me from attending it.

The local youth centre was a run down place in dire need of some TLC.

'Council have been promising us cash for a refurbishment since time immemorial,' Mr Dickins said crossly as he pushed coins into a heavily vandalised vending machine. He was dressed in his civilian clothes, a collarless shirt and some brown cords, which were a little too baggy to be cool. 'I'll be pushing up daisies before they get round to doing anything though,' he sighed. 'The adage is right, Grace. If you want a job doing properly, you have to do it yourself.'

I nodded. A group of girls I recognised from my history class were standing at the back of the hall chatting. I guessed they too were here to audition. One of them turned round and caught my eye. To my surprise she nodded and smiled. I smiled back.

'Blast, I've put sugar in this damned tea by accident. Here,' Mr Dickins handed me the small plastic cup of hot tea and began putting more coins into the machine. 'You see, the children round here, they've got nowhere to go, nothing to stimulate their brains. That's why there's so much crime. Boredom. I tell you, boredom is at the heart of it all.' It was clearly a subject he felt passionate about. 'Fund-raising, Grace,' he continued, gesticulating wildly, the contents of his second plastic cup threatening to spill over. 'The proceeds from the play will go towards getting this place looking half-decent again. We'll need to sell lots of tickets.'

'PR!' I said. 'Some good publicity is what we'll need. Maybe we can invite the local paper down to take some photos. We could produce some great posters and start distributing them to all the parents to put up in their windows and cars and work noticeboards, that sort of thing,' I wondered if I might be able to persuade JJ to design them.

Mr Dickins smiled at me brightly. 'Marvellous ideas, Grace,' he said as he took a slurp of his tea, spilling a few drops on his shirt. 'Let's discuss it at school tomorrow.' He turned away from me towards the eager crowd that had now gathered. 'Right then, folks,' he clapped his hands together. 'Are we ready to rock and roll?'

After the audition, I took the long route home. I couldn't stop thinking about JJ and our kiss, and what it meant. In Oxshott it would have meant we were officially seeing each other, but I wasn't in Oxshott any more – that much I *was* sure of. I let out a long sigh and wondered why something so simple and lovely as an unexpected kiss has to complicate everything so much. But little did I know that things were about to get a whole lot more complicated.

# Chapter 13

On Friday I finally got to see JJ. He was waiting for me over by the bench in the pardon as agreed via text message earlier that day. I could hardly contain myself. I'd been waiting to thank him in person for the Piccalilli piece all week. A text message just couldn't convey how touched I had been.

As soon as I saw him I began waving like an idiot. He smiled back, his hands stuffed in the pockets of his baggy jeans. It was cold outside and he was wearing a kind of knitted woolly hat, which made him look a little like one of those fashion models you see in glossy men's magazines (i.e. pretty bloody gorgeous). I wanted to run over and throw my arms around him, kiss him all over his face and thank him properly for the spectacular picture of my beloved horse, but I didn't want to embarrass him, so I just gave him the biggest smile that I could and hoped he could tell just by looking at me how happy I was. He was smiling too, a little coyly, as I approached him.

'Oh JJ,' I said, 'the painting. It's the most amazing, beautiful thing anyone has ever done for me.'

His smile widened. 'You liked it then?' he said, his green eyes shining even more brightly than usual. 'Did I get the colour right and everything?'

'Perfect,' I said. 'I *loved it*. Thank you.'

'Well, when you said how much you missed him,' he said softly, 'I thought, I can't bring him back to you, but this way at least you can wake up and see him every day.'

I moved closer towards him and he opened his arms a little to receive me. I slotted into them, putting my hands in the back pockets of his baggy jeans and snuggled in close to his warm chest. He smelled of freshly washed clothes.

'Mr Dent is wrong,' I said. 'You're the most thoughtful boy I've ever met. Actually, you're the most thoughtful *person* I've ever met, regardless of the fact you're a boy.'

'You make me want to be thoughtful,' he said, smiling. 'And you're the only girl I've ever met who has ever made me feel that.'

I looked into his eyes. 'Really?'

'Really. Oh God, I almost forgot! How did the audition go yesterday?' he asked. 'Should I get your autograph now before there's a stampede?'

I elbowed him playfully. 'Actually, it went rather well. Guess what?' I said, the smile on my face spreading to a full-on grin. 'I got the part of Desdemona in the school play!'

'You did! See, knew you would!' He hugged me tightly. 'Congratulations! You're going to be a star!'

'Noo,' I said, feeling myself flush as I thought about that day at school. I had got in early just to see if the cast list had gone up on the noticeboard. It hadn't. There was no sign of it at lunchtime either. By afternoon break I had all but forgotten about it, until Candice Dunlop came running into double maths and blurted out excitedly, 'Cast list's just gone up!'

I'd had to wait a full ten minutes for maths to finish, which was torture, before I could go and see if I'd won a part. I held my breath as I approached the noticeboard, my heart beating in my chest like a caged animal. Fighting my way through the small crowd of people, I stood on tiptoe and craned my neck to get a better look.

'Well done,' a girl smiled as she walked past, followed by another, 'Good on you!'

I thought they must be talking to someone else. I scanned the list from the bottom up. For a split second my fluttering heart almost sank when I couldn't see my name anywhere. Then I came to the top and my heart nearly stopped completely when I saw that not only was I on the list, I was at the very top of it! *Desdemona: Grace Foster-Bryce.* I read it twice just to make sure my mind wasn't playing tricks on me. I bit my lip and let out a small squeal of delight. *I* was going to play Desdemona!

'Let's go and take a closer look at Piccalilli,' I said excitedly, taking his hand to pull him away. I was desperate to see the painting up close. He pulled me back again.

'What's the rush?' he said softly. 'There's something I want to say first.'

'What's that?' I asked, the shadows from the branches of the tree dancing across his face, which was perilously close to mine now.

'Well, *do* rather than say,' he said, raising his eyebrows as his lips brushed against mine.

We walked slowly through Sometime Place – the pardon – holding hands, just like a proper couple.

'You'll have to climb the wall if you want to see it up close,' JJ said of the painting. 'Don't be offended, but something tells me you're not the climbing type – at least not in those shoes!'

I looked down at my cream boots with the ties on the side. They only had a dinky heel by my usual standards but they were still not ideal for scaling walls.

'I'll manage,' I sniffed indignantly. 'I was in the Brownies *and* the Girl Guides, you know.'

As we approached the skate park, I noticed a gaggle of people standing around in a group. Puffs of smoke filled the air above them, peppered with their loud voices and the occasional shriek. It was beginning to get dark but her face (and voice) was unmistakable. It was Janice 'gob on a stick' Brady. JJ had spotted the group too and was looking a little apprehensive. I felt sure he slowed his pace.

'Let's take the long route round to the railway, shall we?' he said suddenly. 'The scenic route.' He started to steer me quickly in the opposite direction.

'Steady on,' I gasped, 'what's the hurry?'

'The sun's going down,' he said. 'You won't be able to see the piece properly if we don't get there soon.'

He had a point, only I couldn't help but worry that his haste had more to do with wanting to avoid being seen

holding hands with me. We approached the grassy bank
that ran behind the railway and JJ looked up at the
wall.

'Well,' he said, gesturing towards it, 'ladies first.' I
gulped. The wall was much higher than it looked from
my bedroom window.

'I don't think . . . I didn't realise it was this high,' I
stammered. I'd need a pole vault to get over it.

'Are you sure you want to do this?' JJ asked, looking
concerned.

'Absolutely,' I said unequivocally. My house was
visible from behind the wall and, even though there was
a risk that Mums would look out of an upstairs window
and catch us, I was desperate to see the piece he had
painted up close and I didn't want him to think I was just
some totally feeble girl who couldn't even climb a six-
foot wall.

'I'll go first and then I'll help you over,' JJ said. 'It's not
really as high as you think.' Before I could blink away
my nerves, he had hoisted himself up and over the wall in
one swooping and rather impressive move. 'See!' he said
from behind the wall. 'Try and get a foothold on one of
the bricks and pull yourself up,' he suggested, in the way
that only someone who climbs walls on a regular basis
could. 'Once you're on top of the wall, I can give you a
hand down.'

'OK,' I squeaked nervously, wiping a bead of
perspiration from my forehead. I raised my leg and
attempted to cling on to the wall but I slipped right back
again, almost tearing a nail. So much for my Girl Guide

training. I tried again but the same thing happened.

'Are you OK?' he called out.

'I'm fine,' I lied, grateful that he couldn't see me.

'Do you want me to come and get you?'

'Nooo,' I replied, indignant. I was determined to conquer it. I took a deep breath and a run up, and suddenly I was hoisting myself up on to the top of the wall, wobbling like a demented jelly as I went.

'Ta da!' I said, sitting on top of the wall triumphantly, feeling terribly pleased with myself. 'I did it!'

'Yay!' JJ laughed as he held out his arms to me. Still shaking, I closed my eyes and jumped into them. So there we were, standing together, him with his arm protectively round my waist on the grassy bank of the railway. It was a little steep and I had to dig my heels in to stop me from slipping. I wondered how on earth JJ had managed to paint at such an awkward angle without sliding down the verge. I turned towards the painting and marvelled at the attention to detail as I saw it up close for the first time. Piccalilli even had a diamond encrusted bridle and saddle with the initials GFB on it.

'Wow,' I breathed, which didn't go any way to conveying just how impressed I was. A train hurtled past at speed, sounding its horn. We were closer to the tracks than I had realised and my heart leaped into my mouth. JJ pulled me near to him and I stayed there for a few seconds until the train had passed, and then a few more, just because it felt so nice being in his arms. I looked across the tracks and saw the soft glow of lights coming from my house. It was strange to think that

Mums and Cal were inside.

'Come on, let's walk up this way a little,' JJ suggested. 'There's more room up here. We can sit down.'

I followed him up the steep bank covered in patchy grass and weeds and we huddled together on the cold, hard ground.

'How are things with your mum?' JJ asked.

I snuggled into him even closer and felt the warmth of his body against mine. 'Oh, well, you know. We don't really talk much,' I said. 'Not about anything important, anyway. She went to visit my dad the other week.'

JJ looked at me. 'You didn't want to go with her?'

'I'm not allowed.' I said. 'They decided it was "for the best" that Cal and I didn't visit him in prison.'

'And is that what you want?' JJ said.

I thought for a moment. 'Yes. No. Oh, I don't know. Maybe.'

He gave my waist a little squeeze. 'What is he like, your dad?' he asked, quickly adding, 'Tell me to bog off and mind my own business if you don't want to talk about it.'

'No. No, it's OK,' I said softly. Truth is, I was quite glad he had asked. Mums and I found it difficult to talk about what had happened, so it was good to be able to share my feelings with someone else. 'Dad was, *is,* well, a character I suppose,' I said, smiling. It was the first time I had allowed myself to think of him without deliberately trying to scrub him from my mind. 'He wears a cravat and likes to smoke huge fat cigars.'

'What's a cravat?' JJ asked.

'It's a fancy neck tie, like a cross between a normal tie and a scarf,' I explained, even though I wasn't entirely sure myself. 'He knows a lot about art, obviously.'

'Obviously,' JJ agreed.

'And he is very cuddly and warm,' I said, suddenly feeling sad. It had been so long since I had hugged my dad. In fact, I wasn't sure I could recall the last time we had hugged. I broke my melancholy thoughts for a moment and turned to JJ. 'He was, *is* a wonderful person really. He is kind and friendly and would never see anyone he knew or loved come to any harm.' JJ had hold of my hand now and brought it up to his lips. 'I don't know why he did it,' I said. 'How he got us *all* into such a mess. It was just the biggest shock. I mean, if you ever met my father you would never think there was a criminal bone in his body.' I shook my head. 'I can't help resenting him for everything that's happened. If he hadn't done what he had done then we would still be living in our beautiful home and I would still be riding my beloved Piccalilli, not simply looking at a cartoon painted version of him. Not that it isn't the most amazing, fantastic, cartoon version ever,' I added, not wanting to sound ungrateful.

JJ smiled. 'Perhaps,' he said, 'but there again, looking at it another way, you could say if your dad hadn't done what he did, then you would never have had such an amazing life in the first place. Maybe he struggled to keep it up but didn't want to let you all down.' He shrugged.

I glanced at him. Was that the reason? Had Dad run into financial trouble and turned to crime just to keep us in the life to which we had become accustomed? The thought had never really struck me before. 'So it's *our* fault he's in prison and we're poor then?' I snapped.

JJ grasped my hand even tighter. 'Chill out, narkey knickers,' he said. 'Of course I'm not saying it's your fault. I'm just looking at it from a different angle that's all.'

'Well you can keep your different angles to yourself, if you don't mind,' I sniffed, annoyed by the fact that I was annoyed. 'And don't call me narkey knickers!'

'Whatever you say, m'lady,' JJ said, bowing his head majestically. 'Anyway, personally, I'm glad your old man did what he did.'

I shot him a horrified look. '*Glad*?'

'Yeah. If he hadn't gone and got himself into bother then you would never have come here and I would never have met you.'

I supposed he had a point. 'Mums won't have a bad word said against him,' I said. 'Even after everything that's happened.'

'I guess that's true love for you,' JJ surmised. 'When you truly love someone, you can forgive them anything.'

'Yes,' I said, pulling at the grass beneath me. 'I guess so.' It felt odd to think of my parents being *truly* in love. I wondered if Mums felt the same things that I had begun to feel about JJ. Did her heart skip a beat whenever she saw my dad? Did her tummy do somersaults when he held her hand or kissed her lips even after all these years? Did she spend every waking moment of the day thinking about him? I'd never given much thought to my parents as two human beings who couldn't bear to be apart from one another – they were just my parents and, quite honestly, it was a bit of a gross thought. Suddenly though, sitting next to JJ, watching as the stars began to peep out like tiny holes in the black sky, I realised that's exactly what they were – human.

'Come on,' JJ said, pulling me up from the ground and away from my thoughts. 'Let's go to Café Porto on Goldborne Road. It does the best cheese and ham toasties I've ever tasted and I don't know about you, but I'm freezing my butt off!'

# Chapter 14

It was deliciously warm in Café Porto. Steam from the coffee machine hissed into the air and the waft of bubbling cheese filled my nostrils and awoke my taste buds with a passion. JJ bagged us a table at the back of the café away from the hustle and bustle and went to place our order. I watched him as he nodded and greeted an array of familiar faces in the queue.

'JJ, *ciao*, how are you? What can I get you, my friend?' asked the Italian-looking man from behind the counter. As JJ placed our order of two cheese and ham toasties, a cappuccino for me and a tea for him, I noticed the Italian man staring at me.

'*La signorina è carina*,' he said, smiling at JJ. 'The young lady is pretty.'

JJ smiled and winked at me. I smiled back through my blushes, and looked around at the busy café full of people in winter coats, sipping steaming cups of frothy stuff, chatting animatedly. The pictures on the walls of Italian villagers in fishing boats were old and faded, yet the laughter in their faces appeared untarnished with age.

'I don't suppose you have forty-seven pence?' JJ suddenly appeared at the table carrying a tray with our toasties and drinks. 'I seem to be a bit short,' he said, clearly embarrassed. I felt terrible. I hadn't even offered to pay for my own food!

'Of course,' I spluttered, rifling around my bag for my purse. Why was it always at the bottom when I needed it most? 'Just a sec.' I handed him a five-pound note. 'Please take it,' I said. The last thing I wanted him to think was that I expected him to pay for me, even if I was used to it.

'I said fifty pence, not a fiver,' JJ said, looking a little affronted. 'I think I can manage to buy you a sandwich and a coffee,' he said, 'just about.'

'Well, it's my turn next time,' I said.

'Hey JJ,' a boy said as he walked past our table. 'What's up, man?' He gave JJ a high five and nodded at me. 'All right, babe?' he said in a friendly, thick cockney accent. I smiled back.

'Who was that?' I asked JJ when I was sure that the boy had gone.

'Dave Biggs, local lad. Lived on Hamlet for years. Got his own place now just down the road near Harrow Road. Council set him up with it. It's not a bad little gaff.'

'Do you know *everyone* who lives in Hamlet Tower? I asked.

JJ shrugged. 'I guess so,' he said. 'But then you would too if you'd lived here all your life and seen the same faces day in, day out for the past eighteen years. Hamlet's a community; everyone knows everyone, it's not just me.' His phone beeped. 'Sorry,' he apologised as he opened it. 'It's Zone.'

'AKA Sid,' I giggled.

'Don't you dare let on I told you his real name,' JJ said,

trying to look serious and not doing a very good job of it. 'He'll murder me!'

'What's it worth for me to keep quiet?' I asked coquettishly.

'Hmm,' JJ pondered. 'How about another cheese and ham toastie?'

'But you said you had no money!'

'I don't,' he said, 'but you have!'

I mock gasped. 'Cheeky!'

'Anyway,' he said, snapping his phone shut and giving me his full attention. 'That geezer you saw just now, Dave. He reckons he can get me on the list for a place on his estate, you know, my own flat and that.' He looked quite excited.

'Oh,' I said, 'that's great . . . but I thought you wanted to get away from estate life?'

'I do, I do,' he said, the melted cheese forming strings as he took a bite of his sandwich. 'It would be a start though and, once I've made my fame and fortune in the world of street art, I can buy back Embers and you can live there again, or maybe we could live in a big house together with a swimming pool and games room and tennis courts. Stuff it, we'll have an ice rink too, and a stadium and a helipad and anything else money can buy!'

I smiled. *He wanted to live with me?*

'Besides, you've seen what it's like at Ma's. There's no room to swing a guinea pig in there and, you know what, I'm getting to the point where I'd quite like some privacy.' His eyes met mine for a second. I felt myself flush.

'What *do* you mean?' I said, pretending to be affronted.

'We'd be able to watch DVDs and eat pizza without

the worry of my hundreds of brothers and sisters bursting in on us,' he said. 'What did you think I meant?'

I looked down at the table. 'Nothing,' I said.

He took my hand. 'Maybe I could invite your mum over for dinner and cook her something really exotic like lobster or – what are those small things that posh people always eat at parties?'

'Canapés?' I said.

'Yeah, those. Maybe she'd be so impressed she'd have no choice but to like me. At least she'd know that I was feeding you well.'

'Which is more than can be said of her!' I added. 'My mum is not the greatest cook, it has to be said.'

We both laughed a little.

'I will talk to her about us,' I promised.

'Hey,' JJ said, soothingly, 'it's OK. You've got enough on your plate right now.'

'You're *too* understanding,' I said, 'and she's not understanding *enough*.'

'She just wants to protect you from things she doesn't understand because she loves you,' he said. 'Maybe if she could see that I want to protect you too . . . for just the same reasons.'

I almost choked on my sandwich. Had he just said that he loved me?

'Don't you want that?' JJ asked casually, looking down at the half-eaten toastie on my plate and squirting tomato ketchup on it before I could answer. I pushed it towards him – my appetite had suddenly deserted me.

'Nice one,' he smiled, taking a bite.

* * *

I was still thinking about what JJ had said in the café as we made our way home He had hinted that he loved me. Only now he was acting like he had never said anything at all, so I was left feeling happy and confused at the same time.

'Winter's definitely on its way,' JJ said, shivering a little as he zipped up his puffa coat, wrapping his arm around me. I snuggled up to him.

'Mr Dickins wants to stage the play at the youth centre to raise money for its refurbishment,' I said. 'Perhaps you could help too?' I gave him my best hopeful look. I knew that rehearsing for a play would devour what little spare time I had left to see him after school and studying. If he got involved, I would be able to spend time with him *and* have a legitimate excuse to give to Mums. It was perfect when I thought about it, if I could get JJ to agree, of course.

'You want me to be in a play?' JJ replied as if I'd asked him to throw himself off a cliff.

'Well no, not if you don't want to be. Maybe you could design the backdrop or something,' I suggested.

He thought for a moment. 'Yeah, why not? It's for a good cause and I guess it means I'll get to see more of you!' He lifted me off the ground a little with one arm round my waist. I screamed.

'I knew you'd say yes!' I said, kissing him on the side of his face. 'You're just a great big softy at heart.'

'Yeah, yeah,' he said. 'Just don't tell anyone.'

* * *

It was 22.17. Mums would start getting worried soon. I sent her a text saying I wouldn't be long and that I was getting a lift home from Jess's dad. It was a lie, and I didn't exactly feel good about it, but it had been such a beautiful evening, I didn't ever want it to end. It might not have sounded like much, sitting on the grassy verge of a railway track and sharing toasties and coffee in a greasy spoon café. I knew it would take more than that to impress my old Oxshott friends. Perhaps it would've taken more to impress me once too, but the night had been perfect and now we were sitting on a bench in the pardon, in the cold clear evening, in silence, looking up at the creamy moon as it lit up the blackness above. I suddenly felt a desperate urge to tell JJ that I was falling in love with him. It was the perfect opportunity, but I was just too scared to say it.

I rested my head on his shoulder and let his soft hair tickle the top of my nose as our cold faces bathed in the milky moonlight. He looked down at me and smiled. Then we were kissing and, as we kissed, I said, 'I love you, I love you, I love you,' over and over and over silently in my head in some crazy hope that maybe he could read my mind.

When I got home, Mums was lying on the sofa surrounded by pots containing dubious-looking pulp.

'Try it, darling, it's a banana, avocado and oat face preparation,' she said stiffly from underneath her fruity mask. 'If it works I'm thinking of selling it at Portobello Market. Boris has made me up some fancy labels on his computer and everything!' She sounded excited and I felt happy that she seemed in such good spirits. 'We can always eat it on toast or something if it's no good.'

'That's great, Mums,' I said enthusiastically. I'd never thought I'd see the day when Mums mashed a whole banana into her face but nothing surprised me anymore. 'I'll try some before I go to bed,' I promised, bravely dipping my finger in one of the pots and licking it. It tasted surprisingly better than it looked.

I went upstairs, but I was too charged up with the night's events to even contemplate sleep. I felt I should switch on my PC and write down everything that had happened so that whenever I am feeling down, I can look back and remember the smallest details, the touch of his hand, a certain look, a smile, a kiss, a spoken word, and feel happy again.

A smile swept across my face. I had climbed a wall that evening. Not just physically, but emotionally too.

Later, after I'd heard Mums go up to bed and watched the lights in Hamlet estate turn off one by on, I did something unprecedented: I wrote a letter to my father.

# Chapter 15

♥

I was scared to admit it even to myself for fear of jinxing anything, but, in the weeks that followed, life in London turned out to be better than I could ever have anticipated. For the first time in what felt like an eternity, I was genuinely happy. Although it had been only three months since we had embarked on our journey into the unknown, it had begun to feel as though I had lived on Erwine Street for a lifetime. Oddly, it was a phone call from Legs that really brought it home to me just how much my life had changed. I was pleased to hear her familiar clipped tones as I answered my phone. She sounded breathy and excited.

'Hey Grace, it's me, Legs. Remember?' she said, as if I would have forgotten already! 'How are you, sweetie? I know it's been, like, forever since we last spoke. How's city life? I'll bet you've got a truck load of gossip for me . . .' Before I could begin though, Legs went straight into telling me all about her recent trip to Dubai – her amazing sun tan, her trips on board her dad's friend's catamaran, the lobster lunches and her new Missoni string bikini which drew gasps of admiration from the boys on the beach (even if she did say so herself!).

'So come on then,' she said finally, 'what have *you* been

up to in the past . . . how long has it been since I last saw you?'

There was a pause.

'Three months,' I said, quietly.

'Wow, it feels like yesterday,' she said.

I wondered whether or not I should ask her about Tave.

'I'm sorry I've not been in touch sooner,' she apologised. 'I've just been so busy, what with school and Dubai and my tennis lessons, not to mention all the partying I've been doing lately. You know how it is . . . '

I didn't. Not any more anyway. Everything I had to say felt way less glamorous and exciting, aside from the whole falling in love thing, which I decided not to tell her about. I knew that, even though Legs would be happy for me and find it all dangerously exciting that I was seeing a boy from a bona fide council estate, the others that she would inevitably tell might not. Besides, for the first time in my life I wanted to keep my feelings sacred. They were mine and mine alone. I did tell her about the school play, though, and raising money for the local community centre.

'Oh,' she said, trying to sound enthusiastic. 'That sounds great.' There was another pause. 'Perhaps we can meet up sometime,' she suggested. 'Hang out in Portobello for the day. Do a bit of celeb spotting.'

'I'd love that,' I said, sincerely, even though I think we both knew that it would never happen. Our lives were so different now, and the phone conversation had simply made it all the more glaringly obvious how little we had in common. I hadn't stopped liking Legs. I was grateful that she had made the effort to call me, but her world – a world I knew so well, with its five-star jet-setting holidays and designer spending – suddenly didn't have the same appeal. Here I had purpose: a starring role in a play that would raise money for a fantastic cause, a great friend in Jess, and, most of all, I had JJ.

Despite our contrasting pasts, JJ and I had become closer than ever. It wasn't always easy to see him, especially since Mums insisted on my doing at least two hours' study every evening, but somehow we made time for each other. I felt bad about not telling her about me and JJ, but I figured keeping the truth from someone is not the same thing as a blatant lie. At least that's what I told myself to feel better about it. Besides, it was Mums's own fault I wasn't being honest with her. I knew she'd made up her mind about people from Hamlet estate.

I had been a little more successful in managing to convince Mr Dickins to allow JJ to help out with the school production. I'd stayed behind after English Lit to talk to him.

'I know someone who can paint us a professional backdrop for the play, sir. I think you might know him. His name's JJ. He used to go to Kinsmead and –'

'Jay Jones?' asked Mr Dickins, a look of surprise flashing over his face. 'Is he a friend of yours?'

I felt myself blush a little. 'Yes, sir. He's very talented. I think he'd do a fantastic job.'

'Ah yes, well, I'm not sure.' Mr Dickins shook his head.

'Oh please, Mr Dickins,' I interrupted. 'He's agreed to

give his time for free and everything. He wants to help the cause. I know he had a bit of a reputation when he was here . . .' Mr Dickins raised an eyebrow. 'But he's a different person now. People change. What do you say?' I watched as his expression changed to one of resignation.

'Very well. I'll give him a chance. But it's on your head, Grace.'

I squealed with delight. 'Thanks, Mr Dickins. You won't regret it. I promise!'

It had all worked out quite nicely. Rehearsal nights (Tuesdays and Thursdays) gave JJ and me the perfect excuse, as I had hoped, to snatch a couple of hours together, even if I was sometimes exhausted and cranky, what with trying to cram for impending exams in January and have a love life at the same time. The play was due to show to the public on 6th December, a couple of weeks before we broke up for the holidays, and even though this meant lots of hard work ahead of us, with JJ by my side, I felt ready for any challenge life might choose to throw in my direction. There was just one more thing I needed to do if I were finally to lay my past to rest.


The rain, mixed with the heat of our bodies, had made the window of the train steam up. Instinctively, JJ inscribed his dove tag in the condensation with his finger.

'So where are we going then?' he asked excitedly, sitting next to me and taking my hand.

'It's a surprise,' I said.

He looked at me a little suspiciously. 'Picked a good day for it,' he joked. 'I brought my camera along, just in case.'

It was a wet November Saturday morning. Mums had decided that today she would trial her new range of homemade beauty products down at Portobello Market. She had spent all week whizzing up various fruit and vegetable concoctions in the blender, giving them weird names such as 'loganberry fine-line face mask' and 'cucumber eye-bag-busting lotion' and spooning them into little plastic pots. Boris had even agreed to help her sell them. She had got up extremely early to ensure that she had the best chance of securing a stall down at the market. I watched as the rain crashed against the train window. I felt sorry for them. It was going to be a washout.

The train began to move.

'Here we go,' said JJ. 'Let the magical mystery tour begin.'

I smiled and snuggled into him. 'Mums is setting up her own beauty products business,' I said. 'She's down the market today, selling her lotions and potions with the Russian.'

'She's selling Russian face creams?'

'No, silly,' I giggled. 'They're made of fruit and vegetables. Natural beauty products. She reckons it's the way forward.'

'Quite the little entrepreneur, your mum,' JJ said.

'Yes,' I said, thinking about it. 'I suppose she is. I think she's hoping she'll earn some money out of it so that she doesn't have to take some demeaning job in a supermarket somewhere.'

'What's demeaning about working in a supermarket?' JJ flashed me an indignant look. 'Ma worked in one for years until the twins came along.'

'Oh, I didn't mean . . . I wasn't trying to . . . I don't think that working in a supermarket is bad or anything. It's just that Mums, well, *she* would consider it demeaning. She's never had to work in her entire life. Not officially anyway.'

'Wish I could say the same for my ma,' JJ said, a little sadly.

'Yes,' I said, feeling annoyed with myself. I decided to change the subject. 'The play is less than three weeks away and I still haven't learned my lines off by heart. I know I'm going to be hopeless.'

JJ looked at me nervously. 'I've got a confession to make.'

'Go on,' I said, apprehensively.

'I've been sneakily watching you rehearse.'

I gasped in horror.

'Only once or twice,' he quickly added in his defence. 'I've just poked my head around the door to see you when I've been working on the backdrop. I think you're well brilliant, really I do. You're going to steal the show.'

I felt myself blush. 'You think so?'

'Know so,' he said, sweeping his hair from his eyes. 'You're a star in the making. One day you'll be famous and forget all about me.'

'That would never happen,' I said seriously.

He smiled a little plaintively as he turned to look out of the window. We watched together as the muted greys and browns of London gradually slid into the vibrant, deep greens of the countryside and we were silent for a while as the low hum and soft motion of the train rocked us like a lullaby into quiet submission.

'We're here,' I announced.

'Where's here?' JJ said, shaking himself down a little.

'You'll see.'

JJ duly followed me along the platform and we put our hoods up over our heads to keep off the rain. I watched his expression as he read the station sign: *Oxshott*. He looked at me a little nervously. 'Are you sure you want to do this?'

'I wanted to see it one last time.' I said. 'With you.' He put his arm around my waist and gave it a gentle squeeze in that reassuring way of his, and I squeezed back, grateful.

The little high street looked just the same as it always had. The small parade of shops and the ornate village clock – nothing, it seemed, had changed. Being back gave me such a strange and uncomfortable feeling, like running into an ex-boyfriend – awkward yet familiar. It all seemed so old-fashioned, so quaint and olde worlde compared to London. This place had been the epicentre of my world for so long. Now, it seemed almost impossible to believe I had ever lived there.

We walked through the village and down by the pretty church on Woodshade Road that I had always loved.

There was hardly anyone around, especially for a Saturday – I suspected it was because of the weather. It was a relief in a way. I hadn't come back to be recognised or reconciled with ex-friends and neighbours. I had come back to say goodbye, properly this time. JJ didn't say much as we made our way behind Oxshott Woods. I think he knew where we were heading and chose to let me forge ahead. As the woods began to clear, the tops of the chimney pots and the slates of the vast roof were visible, the tiny attic windows where Cal and I would play as children and look out at the stunning views of the surrounding countryside glinting back at us. My arms started to prickle. I was scared to breathe in case my heart stopped altogether. We stopped in front of the shingled driveway that went on forever. I knew to go any further would be trespassing. I could almost hear the crunching sound of Dad's car making its way along the drive. When I was very small, I would listen out for it – the noise that signified he was home. I closed my eyes and smiled wistfully at the memory.

JJ's mouth was slightly open when I finally looked at him. 'You lived *here*?'

'Yes,' I replied quietly. 'All of my life.'

'But . . . it's . . . it's *huge!*' he stammered, unable to take his eyes from the beautiful house before him.

'I suppose so,' I said. 'Although it only seems huge to me now. It didn't seem so big when we lived here.'

'You could get eight cars on that driveway!'

'Nine actually,' I said.

'And look at all of those windows – there's hundreds

of them. How many rooms did you have?'

I did some quick finger counting. 'Seven bedrooms, four of them en-suite; two cloakrooms, three large bathrooms, a large kitchen diner, two drawing rooms, a huge dining room, a study, a conservatory, games room and a basement. Oh, plus the wine cellar and a utility room.'

JJ stood speechless for a second. 'And outside?'

'Three acres. A swimming pool plus a tennis court. Not that much really.'

'Not that much really?' JJ looked at me incredulously. 'I know you said you lived in a big house but . . . but, well, I suppose I never really thought it would be anything quite as spectacular as this.'

I smiled a little mournfully. JJ was right. Embers *was* spectacular and I was happy that he seemed so impressed with it. It was difficult not to be, after all.

I noticed that whoever lived there now had failed to clip the topiary that Mums was always so pernickety about and it had begun to grow slightly out of shape.

'One of your bathrooms was probably the size of our entire flat,' JJ said in awe. 'I mean, you could get lost in all those rooms. It must've been like living in Buckingham Palace.'

'Not quite,' I smiled at JJ affectionately. 'According to folklore – well, my dad actually – the house once belonged to a very famous highwayman, Captain James Cavalier. He used to tell Cal and me tons of stories about him and his adventures robbing the rich to give to the poor, although I suspect he just made them all up.'

'Wow,' said JJ, moving a little closer towards the driveway. I gently pulled him back.

'They've probably got CCTV,' I said. 'And they can see us from the front drawing room. When I was taking my piano lessons I could see whoever was coming up the driveway.'

'Piano lessons,' JJ whispered. 'Is there no end to your talents?'

I met his gaze. He looked so lovely standing there, slightly damp from the rain, his bright eyes glowing with awe. He leaned in and kissed me ever so softly on the mouth and then he held me in his arms and we kissed some more, deeply and passionately, standing outside Embers, sheltered from the full force of the rain by the surrounding trees. When we finally broke our embrace, I turned to look at my beloved house for one final moment. I blinked back tears and inhaled deeply. It was time to go.

'Let's get an ice cream,' I said as I turned to JJ and smiled brightly.

'In this weather?' he said, looking at me as if I was bonkers.

'All weather is ice cream weather,' I replied, and we walked away from Embers, JJ's first time and my last.

The rain was easing slightly as we sat on a bench in Oxshott Woods, eating our ice creams in silence and listening to the birds chirping in the trees above. JJ had chosen a mint Cornetto and I had opted for a tropical Solero. At one stage we turned to each other and burst out laughing at how odd we must've looked sitting on a soggy wooden bench in the middle of woodland, eating ice cream with our hoods up in the rain. JJ pulled his camera out of his pocket. 'Say ice creeeeeam,' he said, taking a picture of me.

'Noooo!' I yelled, putting my hand up to my face. 'I wasn't ready.'

'They're always the best ones,' JJ said. 'Hey, it's not bad, look.' He started to giggle as he passed me his camera. I was grinning like a mad person, with Solero all over my chin.

'Rot-bag,' I said, disgruntled. 'Let me take one of you.'

'No way, José!' JJ said, pulling his hood over his face.

'Ahh, don't like it now that the boot's on the other foot, huh?' I joked, trying to pull his hood down, which was not that easy considering I was holding an ice cream and trying to take a picture at the same time.

'All right, all right!' JJ said, tired of fending me off. 'But take one of us both, together.' He leaned in close to me and I held out my arm and pushed the button. We were giggling like a couple of kids as we looked at the picture; JJ had his arm round my shoulder and our faces were squashed together. We were both smiling from beneath our hoods and you could just see the top of JJ's ice cream, although it looked more like a surreal green blob, a bit like a small alien's head. Nonetheless, it was a lovely photo and for once I didn't look like I'd been let out of an asylum for the day. I made a mental note to keep it forever.

'Hey, have you got something sharp on you?' JJ randomly asked.

'Like what?'

'I don't know. A metal nail file perhaps?'

'No, I think my mum concealed it in a cake and gave it to my father.' I giggled and JJ did too. 'Silly,' he said nudging me.

I rifled around my bag for something sharp but couldn't find anything other than a half-eaten packet of Maltesers, my lipgloss, keys, a few tampons and a body spray.

'Keys will do!' he said, taking them from me. He began to carve something on the large oak tree behind us.

'Hey, what are you doing?' I shrieked. 'You'll hurt the tree!'

'He can take the pain,' JJ said, his tongue sticking out of the side of his mouth in concentration. 'There,' he said, standing back. He had drawn a big heart and inside were our initials. *JJ & GFB TLA.*

'True Love Always?' I said, raising an eyebrow at him. It was all terribly romantic but was he being serious?

'True Love. Always,' he said as he pulled me towards him by the bottom of my hood.

'I love you, Grace,' he said, his lips cold and sweet against mine and, when we kissed, he tasted of mint choc chip.

On the journey home, JJ and I listened to his iPod, sharing an ear-piece each. Although he was pretty much solely into hip-hop and R&B, there were a couple of softer, more soulful tracks that I quite liked and I rested my head on his shoulder as we let the music do the talking for us. At one point, I looked up at him and noticed he had a desperately sad, troubled look on his face. I took my ear-piece out. 'What's wrong?' I asked.

'Oh, it's nothing,' he said, shaking his head a little unconvincingly.

'No, really,' I said, 'tell me.'

'It was a very brave thing that you did today.' He smiled gently, his dimple only just visible. 'It can't have been easy for you.'

I looked down at the floor. 'Not easy no, but I had to do it,' I said. 'To move on.'

'I'm really glad I came with you,' he said, brushing a few strands of damp hair from my face. The lightness of his fingers made my skin tingle. 'Seeing where you lived, seeing Embers has made me think how very different our lives have been. I mean, I can't even imagine what it must've been like living in such a gigantic house with swimming pools and servants and pianos and stuff . . .'

'Housekeepers, not servants,' I corrected him. 'There's a difference.'

'Housekeepers, servants, whatever . . . you belong in a different world to me. You deserve someone successful, someone rich who can give you everything you've been used to, everything you deserve. I can only just about afford to buy you an ice cream. I haven't even got a proper job.'

Crushed by his self-doubt, I tried to reassure him. 'I can't lie and say it hasn't been difficult. I have missed Embers and everything so much, but believe me when I say I wouldn't swap any of it for all the money in the world. Not now that I've found you.'

'Really?' he said. I could tell he wanted to believe me but couldn't quite let himself.

'If it was a choice between you and going back to live at Embers, even if it meant I got Piccalilli back, I would choose you,' I said, looking straight into his eyes. 'Every time.'

'You can't mean that,' JJ said.

'But I do!' I cried, holding his arms as if by doing so he might somehow believe me.

'I can't offer you anything,' he said. 'But I will make a better life for myself one day, a life you'll want to be part of. I'll make a mint as one of the world's most influential street artists, respected and revered by the graffiti community the world over. I'll be the toast of London, New York and Amsterdam, the street art capitals of the world, you'll see. We'll live somewhere huge like Embers, somewhere bigger than Embers and we'll have ten horses and three swimming pools and . . . '

I put my hand up to his lips to stop him. 'Shhh,' I said. 'The only thing I want is you. Because I love you too – for richer or for poorer.'

We held on to each other for a few moments until a woman sitting opposite us, whom we hadn't noticed, cleared her throat very loudly. Reluctantly, we broke away, trying not to laugh.

'You said you loved me,' JJ whispered in my ear once we had composed ourselves.

I smiled and tried not to giggle. 'And you said you loved me first,' I whispered back.

'I guess that must mean we're in love,' he said, his

hushed tones in my ear sending shivers down my entire body.

'Yes,' I replied. 'I suppose it must.'

On the walk home back to Erwine Street, I asked JJ to post Dad's letter for me. I hadn't had the courage to do it before now and it had been sitting at the bottom of my bag getting dog-eared. He replied that, although he would do anything for me, he felt this was something I needed to do for myself. I knew he was right. I waited a few seconds with my hand half inside the letter box, my fingers stuck to the grubby envelope like glue. JJ gave me an encouraging nod. Finally, I took a deep breath and let it go.

# Chapter 16

Mums's first day as Market Trader Extraordinaire had turned out to be a roaring success. 'We completely sold out of cucumber eye-bag-busting lotion,' she shrieked excitedly as we sat at the kitchen table drinking hot coffee and munching on croissants that evening. 'And one women bought two of absolutely everything. I've made a small fortune! Not bad for my first day at work.'

I was tempted to add 'ever', but stopped myself. It wasn't fair to dampen her spirits with petty sarcasm. Besides, I was glad things were working out for her, for all of us.

'Perhaps you'll come and help me next week?' she asked, her sleek bob still managing to look amazing despite a whole day in the rain. 'Boris was a complete darling, but I did wonder if punters were put off by all that facial hair. You'd make a much prettier assistant.' She was being terribly nice to me. It made me suspicious. 'Oh and, by the way, here's a little something for you,' she said, handing me three crisp ten pound notes. 'I know it's not much, but if things carry on like this we'll be back in the black in no time.'

'Thanks Mums,' I said, giving her a little hug.

'Don't spend it all at once,' she smiled as she began

clearing away the dishes on the draining board. 'So how was your day?'

The truth was, my day had been life changing. It had been both sad and beautiful. I had said goodbye to Embers and 'I love you' to JJ all in the space of a few hours. It had been a day of letting go and moving on and it had been romantic and magical. I couldn't exactly tell Mums any of that though, so I said, 'Nothing to write a postcard about.'

'Lovely, darling,' she answered in that way she does when she's not really listening. 'When is that school play thing of yours happening again?'

'December 6th,' I said, pouring myself another cup of coffee from the cafetière.

'I must write it on the calendar. I'll need to buy tickets for Cal and me.'

Mums seemed impressed that I had won the lead role in the school play, although she was adamant my studies must come first.

'Mr Dickins, my English and drama teacher, thinks I would make a good actress,' I said tentatively, daring to dip my toe in the water.

Mums was standing at the sink with her back to me. 'Don't let him put funny ideas in your head, Gracie,' she said sternly. 'There's no future in acting. Terrible business; all that rejection, never knowing when your next job will be. It's only the lucky few who ever make it, you know. You'd be much better off with a good solid career in medicine or law, something with stability.'

I rolled my eyes behind her back. What was the point

in even trying? I knew she would never listen. Mums pulled back the blind in the kitchen and looked out of the window towards the railway.

'You know I could swear that looks exactly like Piccalilli,' she said, squinting at JJ's artistic homage to my horse. 'Funny.'

I smiled secretly. Lucky for me that Mums was too vain to wear her glasses.

'Grace,' Mums said seriously, turning to look at me. 'I wasn't going to mention anything. I mean, I figured the fact you haven't told me already means you either don't want me to know or it simply isn't true – which I am hoping is the case – but Boris says he saw you down on that hideous Hamlet estate, you know where all the druggies and hoodies live, holding hands with a young man. He said you were kissing.' She sounded remarkably calm. This was not a good sign. 'I told him it couldn't possibly be you because you'd promised me faithfully you wouldn't set foot up there. Besides, no daughter of mine would ever be as common as to stand on some street corner kissing some spotty little oik.'

I didn't dare swallow in case she heard the dryness in my throat.

'I was quite short with Boris about it. He seemed pretty convinced it was you though.'

I carefully put the money back down on the kitchen table and took a large gulp of coffee.

'Do tell me it wasn't, Gracie.' She was blinking at me, her hopeful half-smile beginning to fade in my silence. Typical! I had been spied on – by a Russian!

'Oh my goodness!' Mums put her hands up to her face in horror. 'It's true, isn't it? You really have been on that estate getting up to no good with some delinquent in the street like a common tart!'

'Mums!' I screamed. I had never heard her talk like this. 'If you would just let me explain . . .'

'What's there to explain?' she spat back. 'And there I was, defending you, saying how you would never conduct yourself in such a way with someone from that place when all the time . . .'

'You've never even been on Hamlet estate, Mums,' I said, trying to stay calm. 'How can you judge it so harshly? OK, so it's not exactly five-star living, and yes, it has its troubles, but, you know, some great people live there too. Normal people, people like you and me.'

She bridled. 'You and me? Don't be ridiculous, Grace. The people who live in that hell-hole are nothing like you and me.'

I shook my head. She had made up her mind and that was that. 'His name is JJ and he's seventeen. He's a street artist and I've already met his family   they're amazing *and very welcoming*.' I said, emphasising the last part to highlight the fact that she was the complete opposite.

It seemed to work, because she sat down unhappily and said in a less angry tone, 'JJ? What kind of name is that?'

'It stands for Jay Jones,' I said. 'Please let me invite him round. If you met him, you would change your opinion, I promise.'

Mums buried her head in her hands. 'I knew this

would happen if we came to live here. I said as much to your father. Edgar, I said, the place is crawling with council estates. She'll meet a boy there, I told him, mark my words!'

'Well if it makes you feel any better,' I said, 'thanks to JJ, I wrote Dad a letter and sent it.' Mums looked up at me. 'He thinks Dad did what he did because he loves us, because he only ever wanted the best for us and would do anything to make sure that we got it.'

A fleeting look of surprise crossed her face. 'I suppose he doesn't have a job,' she sighed.

'He's an urban artist,' I said proudly. 'A street painter.'

'Well, that's all right then,' she said sarcastically.

'Please, Mums,' I said, leaning in towards her at the table. 'Please meet him. Then you can make as many judgements as you like.'

She put her china cup down on the table a little too forcefully. 'I must need my head examined,' she said.

I leaped up from the chair, startling her. 'You're going to love him, really you are!' I squealed. I had managed to talk her round! No tears, no screaming matches, nothing! Perhaps the whole letter thing had swung it – whatever, I didn't care.

'Ask him round for Sunday lunch tomorrow,' she said, defeated. 'I suppose he can't be all bad. I have to say I've never seen you this happy before.'

As I raced my way over to Hamlet estate, I though about how familiar the place had become to me over the past few months. The groups of kids kicking footballs against the graffiti-covered walls and zipping up and down on their BMX bikes, the gaggles of teenagers smoking and drinking cider from cans, boy racers leaning out of their beaten-up cars and stereos blasting out gangster rap music – all now seemed far less intimidating than when I had first arrived. Unwelcoming glances had gradually turned into nods of recognition, suspicious looks and a sense of not belonging had slipped into vague smiles of acceptance. Now that I was going out with JJ and people had seen me around, I was no longer a threat, an outsider. I still wasn't quite one of them but I was all right – I was *with* one of them, and that was enough to ensure I was left alone.

JJ was standing with a group of people by the communal rubbish bins when I caught sight of him. I only realised that one of the group members was Janice Brady when I got closer. What was he doing hanging out with *her*? He walked towards me as he saw me approaching.

'You're never going to believe it!' I panted excitedly. Mums has invited you over to Sunday dinner tomorrow!'

JJ looked behind him, a little nervously.

'Look, it's your posh girlfriend,' Janice said to him in her usual snide tones. I suppose it was too much to ask for *her* acceptance.

'The Russian saw us kissing and Mums asked me about it and I told her everything and now she wants to meet you!'

JJ shuffled me away from the crowd. He looked a little embarrassed.

'All right, babe,' Zone called out to me, swigging from

his cider can. I noticed one of the Dulcie twins was looking at me and smirking. His beady eyes and ratty-face twitched at me, making me feel uneasy.

'Hi, Zone,' I called back. 'How are you?'

'Magic,' he said, smiling, 'sweet as a nut, babe.'

'So are you going to come?' I looked at JJ with nervous excitement.

Janice sniggered.

'Um, yeah, well. Er, I'm not sure what's happening tomorrow, Grace,' he stammered, dragging me away.

I felt a little cross. I had made my way over especially to break the good news to him in person and this was his half-hearted response.

'Well, don't sound too enthusiastic,' I said, huffily. Didn't he realise what a breakthrough this was for us?

Once we were safely out of ear-shot from the rest of the gang, JJ kissed me and said, 'That's brilliant news. I'd love to come. How did you manage to get her to agree to it?'

This was more like the reaction I had hoped for, but it felt too little too late.

'I don't know,' I said quietly. I was still too confused and upset by what had just happened to be able to think properly.

'Sounds great,' JJ said. 'Should I dress up or something? I think I've still got my old school tie lurking in the back of my wardrobe somewhere.'

'Just come as you are. We'll expect you for one p.m.' I said. 'I'll see you then.' I turned to leave.

'Aren't you staying?' JJ said, looking surprised. 'It's

Saturday night after all. I thought we could maybe go up to Notting Hill, hang around and grab a McDonald's or something? Don't say I don't know how to treat a girl.'

'I'm on my way to meet Jess,' I lied. 'I'll see you tomorrow.'

'Oh, OK,' he said.

'One p.m.,' I repeated, as I headed in the opposite direction, trying to hold back the tears that had formed behind my eyes. 'Don't be so stupid, Grace,' I said underneath my breath. 'Get a grip. He said he'd come, didn't he?' He hadn't exactly jumped for joy though, I thought miserably as I skulked off, angrily wiping away a fat tear that had escaped and rolled down my cheek.

# Chapter 17

On the way home I called Jess to explain what had just happened. I needed to talk.

'Get your ass over to mine,' she said. 'Oh, and bring chocolate. Lots of it. I've a feeling this could be a long one.'

Jess's bedroom was bigger than my boxroom bedroom, but then again, that wasn't exactly difficult. It was messier too, with discarded coffee cups scattered around and clothes strewn over the backs of chairs. She had a collection of fit movie-star posters, which could have seemed a little babyish, but there were so many of them (one was so big it covered the whole wall) that you couldn't help but be impressed. She also had lots of Betty Boop stuff, the 1950s cartoon character, which I had to admit did look pretty cool, even if her colour scheme was a little too pink for my taste. I sat down at her dressing table, littered with lipglosses of all colours, half-empty eye shadow palettes and various perfume bottles as well as her reading glasses and mobile phone.

I fiddled with a lipgloss lid, worried.

'He was embarrassed by me,' I said, miserably, opening a family-size bag of Revels and taking a handful. 'I turned up unexpectedly and he was there, with Janice

Brady and her delightful chums. I surprised him and he wasn't that pleased to see me.'

Jess looked on sympathetically, eyeing the Revels bag. I passed it to her.

'It's not the first time I've felt a funny vibe,' I went on, chewing on a coffee cream. 'There've been other times when we've been together and he's done a quick U-turn as soon as we've seen a group of his friends. It's like he's ashamed to be seen with me.'

'Yuk, why do I always get the orange creams?' Jess spat, pulling a face.

I raised an eyebrow as if to say, 'Are you actually listening to me?'

She sighed and sat up in her bean bag, which took a couple of attempts. 'You've got to understand, Grace,' she explained, 'JJ is an estate boy and you're a posh girl from the home counties. It's a miracle you've even managed to get it together. I mean, usually, boys like JJ stick to their own kind. It's a class thing. Associating with someone posh, it's almost looked upon as some kind of betrayal or something stupid like that.' She popped another Revel in her mouth. 'Ah, the chocolate one. That's more like it. Listen,' she said, 'it's like I said. He's Danny Zucco and you're Sandra Dee. The hard boy from the wrong side of the tracks and the prim, upper-class goody-goody. You're bad for his street cred.'

'Tell it like it is, Jess,' I said, 'why don't you?'

She flashed me a chocolatey smile. 'Listen, JJ's got an image to protect. Image is everything where he comes from. That's how you survive. And now you've come along and put a spanner in the works. Coming up to his turf like that and saying "Mummy has invited you for tea" is hardly going to fit in with his cool persona, is it? People look up to him, they think he's hard and cool and street, but underneath he's deeply in love with you and is as soft as this coffee cream I'm about to eat. God, it's soooo romantic I could just die!' She sighed again. 'If I don't throw up first that is!' She giggled, and I couldn't help but join in. 'Try not to freak out too much,' Jess concluded. 'You know what boys are like in front of their mates.'

I suppose I should have thought twice before barging over to JJ and announcing Mums wanted to meet him. I had been so excited that she'd actually said yes, and I'd thought that, now we were official and everything, he wouldn't have cared what people thought. Anyway, I took Jess's advice and tried not to worry about it too much. Mums had agreed to meet him and for now, that was all that mattered.

It was all going stupendously well, almost *too* well. JJ had arrived at 12.55 on the dot and had even brought Mums a bunch of flowers from the petrol station down the road. Despite being more accustomed to hand-tied blooms, she accepted them graciously and had thanked him for 'the lovely thought'. JJ had made an effort with his clothes too, swapping his usual skater-boy attire for a more formal outfit of smart(ish) jeans, a stripy shirt and suede desert boots. I felt so proud of him. He clearly wanted to make a good impression.

'It's very nice to meet you, Mrs Foster-Bryce,' he said,

shaking Mums's hand. His voice was slightly wobbly and higher-pitched than usual. It just made me want to hug him.

Cal offered to take JJ's denim jacket and immediately asked him if he wanted to come and see his collection of war memorabilia.

'Cool, I'd love to,' JJ said, smiling at Cal.

'Let our guest sit down first, Cal,' Mums said, 'I'm sure he'll be delighted to have a look after we've eaten. I've cooked roast lamb. I do hope that's OK with you. Grace didn't mention you were a vegetarian or anything so I presumed . . .'

'That sounds great,' JJ said. I squeezed his hand as he sat down at the table.

Mums had laid the vintage china and cutlery and I had even caught her giving it a little polish. I knew that secretly she wanted to make a good impression too.

'Grace tells me you are one of six,' Mums said, bringing the meat to the table and beginning to carve.

'Six!' shrieked Cal. 'Wow, that's a lot of brothers and sisters.'

Mums gave Cal one of her glances. He shut up immediately.

'Yes,' JJ said, looking at me for some kind of reassurance that he was doing OK. 'Two brothers and three sisters. Two of my sisters are twins,' he said.

Mums began spooning slices of lamb on to the warmed plates. It actually looked edible. I could have died when she went on to ask, 'So you all share the same father?'

'Yes,' JJ replied, seemingly unfazed by her impertinent

question. 'My dad's no longer with us though.'

'Oh!' said Mums. 'How long ago did he leave?'

I felt like kicking her under the table, but she was too far away. 'He didn't leave, exactly,' JJ said quietly. 'He died of a heart attack five years ago.'

'Oh,' Mums repeated. 'I am sorry.'

'It's OK,' JJ replied casually. 'I didn't know him that well.'

'Really? Why's that?' Mums asked. How embarrassing. She was being so personal!

'Well, er . . .' JJ shifted in his seat. 'He spent a lot of time, er, away from us.'

'That must have been tough on your mother, what with six children to take care of,' she said, trying to be sympathetic.

'It was,' JJ replied. 'But my ma is a tough cookie and, well, she loved him very much so she always forgave him for any misdemeanours. She says that's how she ended up with six kids, she was *far too* forgiving.' JJ laughed a little too loudly. I wanted the ground to swallow me up. He'd alluded to the 's' word, *in front of Mums*. But, just when I thought the pendulum had swung in the direction marked 'catastrophic', Mums did something unprecedented: she started to laugh too.

'Yes,' she giggled, 'she must've been *very* forgiving indeed.'

The rest of the meal, dare I say it, was rather nice. Surprisingly, Mums's roast potatoes had not threatened to crack teeth and the gravy was lump-free. She talked to JJ about his ambitions to become a famous street artist and although I could tell she was just being polite when she said encouraging things such as, 'I have heard you are remarkably talented,' I appreciated the fact that she was making a huge effort. We chatted about the school play and the backdrop JJ was making and she even pretended not to notice when he used his knife and fork the wrong way round to scrape up his peas. After dessert of Eton mess, JJ duly went upstairs with Cal to check out his homage to all things war and I helped Mums clear the dishes away.

'Well, Gracie,' she said, pulling on her floral rubber gloves like a surgeon about to operate, 'he seems a well-mannered, spirited young man.'

I beamed. 'Yes. He is.'

'Remarkable considering,' she said, spoiling it. 'It's good to have friends from all different backgrounds, darling,' she continued in brazen contradiction to her usual mantra. 'It will come in very handy in the world of work, especially if you choose to become a barrister or such like. You'll end up defending lots of people with a similar background to his, so in a way it's good to try and understand where these people are coming from.'

She really was unbelievable.

'These people?' I hissed under my breath. 'What do you mean *these* people? You make it sound like he's from another planet.'

Mums sighed. 'Like I said, darling, I think he's a very pleasant young man, if a little rough round the edges.'

I walked with JJ to the end of Erwine Street. 'It was a pity

I couldn't show you my boxroom bedroom,' I said, not realising how it sounded. 'But you can see what Mums is like, she wouldn't have allowed it.'

'Well, Miss Foster-Bryce, and I thought you were a *nice* girl!' JJ teased.

I felt my cheeks flush red. 'No, no! I meant, I . . . well, I wanted you to see the view I have of the railway and Piccalilli, and of Hamlet Tower. I hoped you might be able to point out your flat.'

'A likely story!' he said, an eyebrow raised.

I gave him a playful nudge. 'Don't, you're embarrassing me.'

He pulled me in close to him by my waist until our noses were almost touching.

'I would have done *anything* to see your boxroom bedroom,' he breathed. 'Perhaps I will get the chance one day.' He kissed my burning cheek softly. 'Your mum – she thinks I'm wrong for you.'

'No,' I shook my head emphatically. 'She thought you were well-mannered and charming. Anyway, who cares what she thinks? I love you and that's that.'

'I love you more,' JJ said.

'Enough to say it in front of your friends?' I asked.

He stopped and looked at me. 'What makes you say that?'

'Nothing,' I said, clearly meaning the opposite.

'Enough to agree to paint a backdrop for your play,' JJ said. 'Or to spend all night in the freezing drizzle spraying you a picture of your horse . . .'

'OK, OK,' I said, rolling my eyes and smiling.

'Your brother is funny,' he said, I suspected deliberately changing the subject.

'He's very much like Dad,' I said, suddenly remembering the letter I had sent him.

We stood back from each other a little. It was time for me to go.

'One day you'll leave here,' he suddenly said. 'I can almost feel it.'

'You can't get rid of me that easily,' I joked.

He shook his head. 'All this, you, me, it's just temporary. Talking to your mum has made me realise it more than ever.'

There was me thinking things had gone so much better than I could have ever hoped for! Now JJ seemed sad and insecure. I suddenly panicked with the thought that he would break up with me there and then, and save himself from what he was convinced would be inevitable heartache later. Damn Mums.

'There's nothing temporary about you and me,' I said unequivocally. 'This is for keeps.'

JJ kicked an imaginary Coke can on the floor, like he does whenever he feels awkward. He lit a cigarette and took a puff. I hadn't seen him smoke in a while. I knew he'd been trying to give up – I sensed for me as much as anyone.

'I think your mum noticed my lighter,' he said a little miserably.

'So?' I said. 'She smokes too. Lots in fact.' I knew what he meant though. Mums had mentioned it to me when JJ was upstairs with Cal. Although she wasn't in any position to criticise him for smoking, as I very quickly pointed out, I knew she was unimpressed. In her eyes, it was OK for the upper classes to enjoy a cigarette or two, but for the lower classes, well, it was a dirty habit. JJ took another drag of his cigarette and then threw it to the ground as if disgusted by it.

'Thanks for today,' he said. His mouth smiled but his eyes looked distant and melancholy. 'I'm sorry.'

'For what?'

'For the fact that your mum thinks I'm not good enough for you.'

My eyes began to well up with tears now.

'I may not have the right background, but I'm determined to have the right future,' he said. 'I'll make her love me.'

'I don't care if she doesn't love you,' I said, blinking tears back furiously. '*I* love you and that's all that matters to me.'

He smiled. 'Oh Grace,' he said, 'you're so gorgeous and smart and eloquent and . . .'

'Since when did you start using words like eloquent?' I teased.

'Since I began eating dictionaries for breakfast,' he replied.

'How could you?' I giggled. 'I thought dictionaries were an endangered species from where you came from.'

'Protected species,' he laughed. 'I'm on the hunt for a tasty thesaurus for my dinner next.'

'Nooo,' I yelped, and we were laughing and holding each other again. The grey mood had passed.

'So, do you want to come and see the view from *my* bedroom?' he said, his green eyes smiling again, mischievously. 'Ma's taken the twins out for the afternoon . . .'

'Well, I have heard it's quite spectacular.' I smiled coyly. 'The view, that is.'

'It is,' JJ said, 'but nowhere near as spectacular as the view I have in front of me now.'

'Flattery will get you everywhere,' I replied, flirting outrageously.

'Everywhere?' JJ enquired.

'Don't push it,' I said, my heart thumping loudly, as we began to walk, hand in hand, in the direction of Hamlet Tower.

# Chapter 18

It was December 6th. The opening night of the school play had finally arrived and to say I was nervous was a spectacular understatement. Tonight was the night all our hard work would hopefully pay off. At the very least, I prayed I would not forget my lines or corpse during the scene when I had to pretend to kiss Jacob Matthews (who played Othello, my husband). It was embarrassing enough having to act this scene in front of the cast and Mr Dickins, not to mention JJ, who wasn't particularly overjoyed that I had to kiss another boy, even if it was only make-believe. 'I guess I'll have to get used to it,' he had reluctantly said. 'After all, when you're a famous A-list star you'll probably have to kiss loads of dead fit Hollywood actors on a daily basis.'

'It would never be as nice as kissing you though,' I had assured him, touched by his jealousy.

I walked along Portobello Road, on my way to the youth centre. Christmas was coming and the world had begun to twinkle and shine. Decorations and smiley Santas adorned the shop windows, making small children squeal with delight as they passed by. Evergreen spruces sold by men with fingerless gloves and bobble hats on street corners filled the air with pine-scented festivity. I smiled contentedly as I watched the hustle and bustle of the market traders packing up for the day.

Rows and rows of antique stalls lined the entire road, the vast array of eclectic wares for sale dazzling me. It had to be the only place in the entire world where you could see an old Victorian washing mangle next to a satellite dish, a string of shiny pearls by a stuffed grizzly bear, or mobile phone covers next to a collection of vintage hat stands. It was the most fascinating, exciting place I had ever seen in my life.

Despite my nerves, I was feeling good. Two days previously, the dress rehearsal for the play had gone insanely well and Mr Dickins was delighted that the tickets had completely sold out.

'At this rate we'll not only be able to give the youth centre a decent re-vamp, we'll have enough left over for new equipment for the children as well! It's marvellous, I say, marvellous,' he'd blathered excitedly.

That day, JJ had unveiled his backdrop to a round of rapturous applause from the cast, led by me. In his own inimitable cool style, he had depicted the play's settings – a Venetian Street on one side of the canvas and Cyprus on the other – with what Mr Dickins described as 'unique charm'.

I had felt my chest swell with pride on JJ's behalf. I knew Mr Dickins had taken a chance on him. JJ didn't exactly have a brilliant reputation among his former teachers at Kinsmead, but he'd proved them all wrong by producing something so breathtaking that they had all had to eat their words.

I held the letter tightly in my hand as I braved the freezing drizzle. I was too scared to open it. JJ had suggested that we read it together after the play had finished over coffee and toasties in Café Porto. That way, if I did get upset, it would not affect my performance. However, my impatience got the better of me and I found myself taking a deep breath and tearing it open as I walked down the street in the rain.

*My darling Grace,*
*To receive a letter from you after all this time has made my heart stand still. When I recognised your handwriting, I ripped open the envelope with all the fevered excitement of a schoolboy at Christmas, my delirium so great I all but tore the letter in two!*

*I realise you are a long way from forgiving your old dad for being such an incorrigible fool but your letter brought me such happiness that I am now filled with renewed hope.*

*I am overjoyed to hear all your news – Desdemona in* Othello, *a role you were born for no less! I know you will play her with strength and presence. She too was never frightened to stand up for her beliefs (or stand up to her father either!). I only wish I were able to watch you, my beautiful daughter, shine like the star you are on that stage. It is of little consolation to you, I am sure, that I will be thinking of you every second on the 6th, just as I have thought of you every second in the time we have spent apart.*

*I am delighted you have found genuine happiness in your new home. I find this a comforting thought amongst my guilt and contrition.*

*And what is this you say about a certain fellow? Do I detect that it is he who is responsible for your sunny state of mind and your change of heart in putting pen to paper? If this is the case then I suggest you marry him right away, though I should run that one by Mums first, won't you? I'm in enough trouble as it is already! All joking aside, he sounds like a remarkable and talented chap. I should hope to meet him very soon, perhaps sooner than you think.*

*I know things have been difficult for you – all of you – since I have been gone. I am looking forward to a chance to put things right again. To be among the family I cherish with all my heart and have missed from the very depths of my soul. I hope you will give me that chance, Grace.*

*Break a leg, my darling.*

*Your ever loving Dad xxxx*

I read the letter twice over, despite the fuzzy rain blurring my vision. I was drawn to the words 'sooner than you think'. Did Dad know something we didn't?

The moment I arrived backstage, I knew something was terribly wrong. Mr Dickins's usual sunny demeanour seemed dark and sombre and it looked as though some of the female cast members had been crying. A horrible feeling of dread engulfed me. I looked at the clock on the wall. It was six p.m. The nativity play that the local primary school children were performing was due to start any minute. I could hear the scraping of chairs as parents arrived to take their seats and watch their loved ones up on stage. Mums and Cal would be here soon too. There was no sign of JJ though. We had agreed to meet backstage at six. He'd said he would help me go over my lines one last time before watching the play from the wings. I hoped he would arrive soon; I needed his support. 'Is everything OK, sir?' I asked Mr Dickins as I took my coat off.

'No, Grace, everything is far from OK,' he snapped. I was a little taken aback. Mr Dickins had never been short with me before. 'Last night someone broke into the office and stole the ticket money. It's all gone, Grace. Five hundred pounds, just like that!' He buried his head in his hands despairingly.

I stared at him in shock. 'Stolen?'

'Yes, and to add insult to injury, whoever decided to take it has defaced the toilets with graffiti. Made a right mess, I tell you, a right royal mess.'

'Oh, Mr Dickins,' I gasped. 'This is terrible.' Tears began to sting my eyes. 'Who would do such a thing?'

He looked uneasily at the floor. 'The police are looking into it. I'm afraid to say they already have a suspect.'

I swallowed dryly. 'Really?'

'I'm sorry, Grace,' he said, even though I wasn't quite sure what he was apologising for.

'So what happens now, sir?' I asked, choking back tears. 'Does this mean we're not going ahead with the performance?'

He straightened himself up. 'Good heavens, no, and let the thief win? Over my dead body. You've all worked so hard for this. The show must go on!'

I felt wretched. Where in heaven's name was JJ? He would be devastated when I told him the news. I decided to text him.

*Where r u? G x*

The low hum of voices was audible from behind the curtain as people took their seats. The nativity play was starting.

'Hurry up, JJ,' I hissed under my breath. At this rate, he would miss the opening act. I tried to stay calm, but I couldn't shake a horrible sense of foreboding.

After twenty minutes and still no text from JJ, I tried calling him. It went straight to voicemail. I left a message. 'JJ,' I whispered into my phone, 'Where *are* you? Something terrible has happened and we're on in ten minutes. Please call me. I'm worried.' I bit my lip. Perhaps he had been taken ill. What if there had been an accident? My mind was beginning to race. I felt sick with panic and fear. I knew JJ wouldn't have missed this performance for all the world. He had worked incredibly hard on the backdrop and knew just how much tonight meant to me. I had half a mind to just run from the stage and try to find him, but I knew I couldn't let Mr Dickins down like that, not after what had happened.

I'm not sure how I managed to get through the performance. Hard as I tried, I just couldn't put my heart and soul into it. I had scanned the audience for his family – they were supposed to come too – but the only faces I recognised were Mums, Cal and Boris, beaming and waving at me distractingly from the seventh row, and Jess right at the back. Despite a standing ovation and rapturous applause – which would have usually made me ecstatic beyond words – I felt numb and empty as the curtains finally closed. The first thing I did when I got backstage was check my phone. My heart almost jet-propelled out of my mouth when I saw there was a message waiting.

*All is not good. Am sorry I missed u. Will xplain all later. Pls 4give me. J x*

# Chapter 19

My heart still pounding, I changed back into my skinny jeans, jumper dress and grey suede boots as cast members congratulated each other backstage. Mums and Cal were waiting for me outside the dressing room door. Mums had tears in her eyes.

'Oh, Gracie,' she said, throwing her arms around me in that dramatic way she does when she knows others are watching her. 'You were . . . you were simply wonderful.' She took a step back and stared at me as if she had suddenly seen me in a new light. 'I had no idea you were such a good actress,' she trilled, proudly.

'Hurmpf,' said Cal. 'How do you think she's managed to get her own way all these years?' I wanted to laugh but the muscles in my face had frozen with worry and fear.

'Darling,' Mums said. 'You were the star of the show. Acted half of the others off the stage, didn't she Cal?'

Cal rolled his eyes and nodded. 'You were all right, I suppose,' he mused. 'Though I would've liked to have seen a more realistic fight scene between Roderigo and Cassio.'

I couldn't bring myself to feel pleased, not without knowing what had happened to JJ.

Mums asked me if I wanted a lift home, but I lied and

told her I would be hanging back with the cast for a bit of a celebration. I didn't mention anything about the money going missing.

'Well, you all deserve to celebrate,' she gushed, 'you were all fabulous. But you were the *most* fabulous.'

Jess was waiting for me outside the youth centre. We were supposed to be meeting up with JJ and Zone for a kind of double-date type thing that night after the performance to celebrate. I had spent ages convincing JJ that Jess and Zone would make a good match and JJ had spent even longer convincing Zone to come out with us. Jess had been looking forward to it – I was sure she'd had a secret crush on Sid for ages.

'Did you hear?' I asked her solemnly. 'Someone broke into the youth centre last night and stole the ticket takings.'

Jess nodded. She looked troubled. 'Listen, Grace, I don't know how to tell you this but JJ's been arrested,' she blurted out. 'He's down at Paddington Police Station on suspicion of theft and criminal damage. They think he did it. They think he stole the ticket money.'

I couldn't believe what I was hearing. Was this one of Jess's jokes? If it was, well, this time, she had gone a step too far. But the grave expression on her face told me otherwise.

'It . . . it can't be,' I stammered.

'Apparently they found a drawing of a dove in the boys' loos. Everyone knows JJ's tag is a dove . . . They're saying he knew where the cash was kept too.'

I screwed my face up in confusion. 'Why would JJ sign

his name on the wall of a place he had just robbed?' I spluttered. 'And we all knew where the money was kept – myself included.'

'Look, if it's any consolation, I don't think he did it either,' Jess sighed. 'And if I ever find out who did, I will ring their sodding necks. This was my first date with someone in over six months and now it's ruined! I swear I'm destined to be a sad singleton for my entire life.'

I couldn't believe she was being so glib. What was a double date with Zone when JJ had been wrongly arrested for a crime I knew he would not, *could not* have committed?

'I want to see it for myself,' I said defiantly. 'This so-called dove, I want to see it.' I marched back into the building.

'Grace, Grace!' Jess ran after me. 'Wait!'

I stomped through the empty hall, pushing chairs out of my path. A red *Out of order* sign hung on the door of the gents' toilets. I ignored it and stepped inside. Thick black marker pen daubed the walls. Wet toilet roll stuck to the mirrors as if it had been thrown in a mindless snowball fight. Then I saw the drawing of the bird in the top right-hand corner. At first glance, the untrained eye could have been forgiven for thinking it was JJ's, but I knew instantly that it wasn't. JJ's dove was his hallmark and it was a beautiful and carefully drawn creation. This bird was crude and basic, a poor imitation.

'Someone reckons they saw him loitering around here last night,' Jess panted as she caught up with me. 'I saw his sister on the estate, she told me everything.'

'But this is not JJ's work,' I said, almost shouting. 'He did not do this. He *would* not do this!' I was incensed at the injustice. 'I have to go to him.'

'No,' Jess said softly, standing in my path. 'If you go marching up to the police station now you'll only make things worse.'

Worse? How could it be any worse? But she was right. Helpless as I felt, the best thing I could do for now was to go home and wait.

I hardly closed my eyes that night. Was JJ locked up in a cold cell, alone and scared? Why hadn't he contacted me? Surely the police would have released him without charge by now, once they realised what a terrible mistake they had made. I had not dared to mention any of this to Mums. I could just imagine the smug 'I told you so' look on her face. As soon as I returned home I had slunk off to my room, explaining that it had been an exhausting day and that I was dog-tired. I couldn't face talking to her, even though, above all people, she should have understood how I felt.

I spent the next morning re-arranging my sock drawer for something, *anything,* to do to take my mind off what might be happening to JJ. Mums had even brought a breakfast of scrambled eggs, toast and orange juice up to my bedroom, but I felt too sick to be able to eat it. I kept texting Jess to see if she had heard any news. She hadn't, but promised faithfully that she would text me if she did. I even toyed with the idea of going over to the estate to speak to JJ's mum. Friendly as Mary was though, I wondered if she might not want visitors at a time like this. Perhaps she was already down at the police station with JJ. Every minute that passed felt like an unbearable eternity. Then my phone finally beeped.

*Meet me at the pardon bench in half an hour. I will xplain everything. J x*

I raced down to Sometime Place and arrived twenty minutes early. I must've looked positively demented pacing up and down the canal bank, so much so that at one point a voice shouted from over the bridge, 'Hey you, lady! Don't jump!'

As soon as I saw him in the distance, I ran to him and he scooped me up in his arms. He smelled fresh and clean, as if he had just had a shower, and he was wearing baggy combat pants and his favourite trainers. I had never felt happier to see him.

'Let's sit down,' he said when I had finally let go of him. 'We need to talk.'

'Are you OK?' I said, tears falling down my cheeks. I quickly brushed them away. 'You *look* OK,' I said tentatively, but when I looked closer I could see that his face was pale and he had dark rings under his eyes.

'I'm fine,' he nodded, unconvincingly.

'What happened?' I asked, taking his hand. It shook a little. I squeezed it tightly. 'I was freaking out when I couldn't see you at the performance. Then Mr Dickins told me that the money had been stolen and about the graffiti and whatnot. It was so much to take in. I mean, I didn't even think for a moment you could have anything to do with it, so when Jess told me that you'd been arrested . . .'

'I felt so bad about not turning up to the performance,' he said, biting his top lip and shaking his head. 'I was desperate to see you, be there with you in your moment of glory, but they came to the flat, the police, yesterday afternoon. There was nothing I could do.'

'They say someone saw you hanging around the youth centre last night,' I said. 'What happened?'

'I *was* outside the youth centre last night, it's true,' he said, 'but not for the reasons they think I was. I'd heard on the grapevine that the Dulcie twins were going to turn the place over. They knew the ticket money was being kept in the building. I'd gone up there to try and stop them from doing anything stupid. I mean, they're only fourteen. They're just kids, not much older than my brothers. I hoped I could put a stop to it but it seems I was too late.' JJ rubbed his hands over his face. 'They must've smashed a window and crawled in through the toilets.'

'They drew a picture of a bird,' I said. 'It looks like they've tried to copy your tag. Why would they do that? It's as if they tried to frame you.'

JJ shook his head. 'It's not like that,' he said softly. 'They look up to me. They're always hanging around, asking to come and watch me paint. I think they did it as a kind of tribute. They wanted me to be impressed.'

'Some tribute!' I spat. 'Thanks to them, you've been wrongly arrested. Still,' I said, 'you obviously told the police all this, right?'

JJ shifted on the bench a little. 'Well, no, not exactly.' he said.

'Not *exactly*?' I said, my voice rising again.

'Not at all, in fact.'

I stared at him in disbelief. 'Let me get this straight. You know that the Dulcie twins stole the money and vandalised the youth centre, right?'

'They've stashed the money in their flat, apparently.'

'So why haven't you told the police?' I screamed. He wouldn't look at me. 'They would have released you once they found the money. You might've even made it to the performance on time.'

'It's not as easy as that, Grace,' he said, so calmly it made me want to shake him. 'I can't grass them up. It's not what we do round here. You don't rat on your own.'

I stared at him, incredulous. 'They're hardly family, JJ,' I spluttered. 'They just happen to live on the same estate as you, in the same way as the Russian lives in the same street as us. It doesn't mean that if I found out he had stolen the money I wouldn't tell the police!'

'You don't understand,' he said wearily. He was right, I didn't.

'They took money that was supposed to be used for making the youth centre a better place for local children,' I said. My face was burning and I felt sick with rage. 'I can't believe you're defending them!'

'I agree with you, really I do,' JJ said. 'What they did was wrong and I can only hope that somehow the police find out they've got the wrong dude and that the Dulcies get caught and pay for what they did.' He bowed his head again before quietly adding, 'But it won't come from me.'

I shook my head in anguish, unable to comprehend what I was hearing.

'Do you know what they do to people who grass round here, Grace?' JJ looked up at me and took both my hands in his. 'They shove dog poo through your letter box, chuck petrol bombs through your windows and spray *Rat Scum* in huge letters on your front door. They spit at you in the street, harass your family, hound you out. You see, when you come from an estate like Hamlet, when you grow up on the breadline with nothing, you do what you can to survive. Loyalty is the only thing that unites you. You look out for each other. You keep an eye open. If the police come knocking, you know nothing. And you never, never grass. *That's* the law, Grace. That's *Hamlet* law.'

'Yeah?' I snapped, shaking my hands free, 'well that's the most ridiculous law I've ever heard! Are you seriously saying that *you're* prepared to take the consequences for *their* actions? You're happy for everyone to think that *you* stole that money? That you're nothing but a low-life thief and a vandal when you're anything but? And what about your mum?' I was shrieking now. 'You promised her you would never get into trouble again. That you wouldn't end up like your father and disappoint her. What will she think? Don't you care?'

'Of course I care!' JJ was yelling too. I had struck a nerve. 'The people what know me, know the truth, that's all that matters.'

'It's *who*,' I spat. 'It's the people *who* know me.'

JJ looked down at the floor again and I instantly hated myself.

'I don't condone what they've done, Grace,' he said quietly. 'But I can't shop them to the cops. I just can't.'

'But you *have* to tell them!' I was half on my knees in front of him now, begging. 'You'll go to prison, locked away for something you didn't do!' It was bad enough my dad being locked away for a crime he *had* committed, but for JJ to be thrown in jail when he was innocent . . . 'Well, if you won't tell them,' I said, 'then I will! I'll go to the station and tell them the truth right now.' I got up to leave.

'No!' JJ panicked, grabbing my arm. 'Promise me, Grace,' he said, locking my gaze. 'You can't say anything. You're *my* girlfriend, we'll both get it in the neck if you do. Your family too. Is that what you want?'

'Of course not,' I sighed, dropping back down on to the bench. 'But there must be another way to stop this.'

'Trust me, there isn't,' he said, hopelessly.

'I can't believe the twins haven't come forward,' I said. 'They're obviously happy to let you carry the can for what they've done. I mean, where's the loyalty in that? Surely that's frowned upon as much as being a grass?'

JJ shook his head. 'I'll come back from prison a hero,' he said.

'Well, whoopee,' I sneered. 'A criminal record that could affect the rest of your life, not to mention the emotional scars of time in prison, but hey, it's no biggie because on Hamlet estate, everyone will think you're the bee's knees.' I snorted in derision.

JJ cast his eyes to the floor. 'I don't expect you to understand.'

I glared at him. 'Understand?' I scoffed. 'How can you possibly expect *anyone* to understand the logic in that? It's pathetic!'

'It's just the way it is.' His voice was almost a whisper. 'I'm sorry.'

I burst into tears, unable to keep it all in any longer.

'Please Grace,' he said, putting his arm around me. I pushed it away. 'Does this change the way you feel about me?' he asked, his voice thin. 'I'll understand if you say yes.'

I looked up at him, his flaxen hair freshly washed and a little fuzzy in the dampness of the air. The truth was that, despite the horror of the situation, the mindless madness of 'Hamlet law' and the nightmare that I suspected lay ahead of us, it didn't change the way I felt about him at all. Not a jot. You see, my love for JJ was that change-your-world kind of love, that rocks you to the core so that you're never the same again. It would take more than a misunderstanding, however steep the consequences, to shake the roots of this tree. I was angry though, angrier than I had ever been in my life. I couldn't believe JJ could just throw his life away like that.

'I have to go,' I said. I needed time to think. I did not dare turn round and look back as I walked away from him, even though it took every last drop of strength I had left in me not to. I knew that it would take just one glance, a flash of hurt in his eyes, and my resolve would collapse like a house of cards.

# Chapter 20

That night I cried myself to sleep, my anger eventually giving way to a world of pain and hurt. I had turned my back on JJ in his moment of need. I had felt so frustrated, so incensed by his misplaced loyalty that at the time I could not bear to even look at him.

I clung to the hope that, following our conversation and a good night's rest, JJ would see sense, turn the Dulcie twins over to the police and clear his name – but deep down in my heart I knew that he never would. In JJ's world, reputation was everything, no matter how high the price. Damn him and that stupid estate where he lived! What kind of 'law' allowed a whole tower block of people to keep quiet about something they knew to be true and let an innocent man take the rap? Every bone in my body told me I should tell the police what I knew, because I felt guilty too, guilty for knowing the truth and doing nothing, and guilty for abandoning JJ when he needed me most.

I chewed on a fingernail, manically tearing at my cuticles. What I needed now was a miracle: a fairy godmother to fly down from the skies, wave a magic wand and make everything right again. And I needed her fast.

At school the next day, JJ and the stolen money was the talk on everyone's lips. Once again, I found myself the centre of attention for all the wrong reasons.

'Controversy follows you,' Jess said. 'It's not your fault, it's just the way you were made,' she decided.

'Thanks,' I said, 'that makes me feel *so* much better.'

'Cheer up,' she said, linking her arm into mine. 'All is not lost yet. Who knows what will happen? Perhaps the police will find some new evidence or something. Chloe Sanders said they've been going round to the houses of everyone who took part in the play and questioning them, you know.'

'Really?' I said. If that was the case, it was only a matter of time before they got to me; after all, I was his girlfriend. An unsettling thought crossed my mind. What if they thought I had something to do with it all, that I was an accomplice? The thought of the police sniffing around asking questions unnerved me. Mums would have to know everything and then there would be histrionics. I could almost hear the chink of the Campari bottle against glass already.

'So have you heard from JJ?' Jess asked. 'Zone said he's really depressed. He thinks you don't want to know him.'

'Oh,' I replied, quietly, letting my head drop. 'When did he tell you that?'

'Last night,' Jess said, carefully. She bit her lip. 'We went for a Maccie D's together.'

'I'm glad you two are getting on,' I said, wanting to be pleased for her.

'We kissed,' she said quietly, adding, 'finally.'

In an ideal world I would have been thrilled to know that she was getting it together with my boyfriend's best pal, because she deserved it and that meant lots of time hanging out together on double dates, having a laugh, just the four of us.

'That's great, Jess,' I said. I couldn't begrudge her happiness in the face of my misery.

Truth was, JJ *had* texted me that morning asking if we could meet. He knew I was still angry with him, and I could tell he wanted to put things right. I had not decided whether to text him back or not. I didn't know if I could face seeing him again, knowing that nothing I said or did would change his mind about telling the truth.

'It's harsh,' Jess said, reading my mind, 'but it's how it works on Hamlet, and on most estates round here, from what I hear. Like I said before,' she smiled at me sympathetically, 'they all stick together.' It was testament to our friendship that she didn't actually say, 'I told you so.'

I was glad to be home. The once uninviting pokiness of the small front room now appeared cosy and welcoming in contrast to the cold outside. I sank down into the sofa next to Cal, who was watching a TV documentary on wildebeest.

'What, no war documentaries?' I half-heartedly teased as I snatched the remote from his grasp and switched over to MTV. It was playing the new video of one of my favourite bands of all time, The Rebekahs (so called because all the girls in the band are called Rebekah).

Their latest song, 'Hopeless', seemed horribly apt.

'There's a war documentary on the History channel at quarter past seven. Mums says I can't watch it though because she "wants to talk to us",' Cal said, miming the inverted commas. My heart almost stopped beating in my chest. Surely the police hadn't been round already? Mums would have called me on my mobile and demanded I come straight home if that had been the case.

'What could have gone wrong now?' I whined nervously.

He shrugged. 'It could always be good news, little Miss Negative.' But even he didn't sound convinced.

'Ah, Grace,' Mums said as she entered the room with a cafetière of coffee and custard creams. Now I really was worried. Coffee *and* biscuits. I braced myself. 'I was hoping you'd be back,' she said, pouring the coffee into three china cups. I felt too sick with worry even to touch the custard creams. 'I need to talk with you both. Now, which do you want first, the good news or the bad news?'

'Bad news!' Cal cried. 'Then the good will seem even better afterwards.' There was some kind of logic to that statement so I didn't argue.

'Well, we won't be having any Christmas decorations this year . . . ' Mums said mournfully. Cal and I waited for her to continue but she didn't. Was that it? Was that the terrible news that had me so panicked? ' . . . because we won't be needing them!' Mums finished, her red, glossy mouth widening into a dazzling smile.

'Why not?' I enquired, slightly irritated by her unexplained euphoria.

'Because we will be at Grandma Violet's!' she shrieked.

'Granny V's! Cool,' Cal said. He seemed genuinely pleased – after all, we hadn't seen her in almost as many months as our absent father, not since she and Mums had had that horrendous row and vowed never to speak to each other ever again.

'So you made up then?' I said, wondering why I didn't feel as pleased as I thought I should be.

'Yes, darling,' she beamed. 'We talked on the phone for hours the other evening and we've resolved our differences once and for all. It's wonderful news, isn't it?'

'Yes,' I said. 'Great. So when are we leaving? And,' I added, more importantly, 'when are we coming back?'

'That's just it, darling,' Mums said ecstatically. 'I don't think we will be coming back! Grandma has kindly offered to let us live in her beautiful holiday cottage down in the Cotswolds until Dad is back with us and we can decide what we want to do from there! Isn't this just the best news we've had all year, poppets?'

Cal ran to Mums and hugged her.

'I knew you'd be happy, Tigs,' she said, her tears leaving tracks in her foundation. 'We'll finally be out of this place. No more London hell for us!' She raised her fist in a triumphant salute. I stood up, stunned into silence. I had not seen this coming. This was worse than a visit from the police.

'What about school?' I said quietly. 'We've just got settled here . . . '

'I've spent all day looking into it and I've spoken to a delightful school in Castle Combe,' Mums said, brushing away a tear of happiness from her face. 'Grandma Violet has even offered to pay for you both to attend a private college, so I'll be looking into that too. I know it's not ideal, all this constant upheaval, but now, thank goodness, you need never go back to that horrid Kinsmead school. There is no point in finishing the rest of term – it would be a waste of time. Grace, you can get on with your revision, and Cal can help me pack up here – there is so much to do!'

My legs began to buckle beneath me. This was a disaster. A few months ago I would've given a kidney to have heard such news. Now I realised I did not want to leave the dirty yet fascinating hubbub of Goldborne Road, or the oddly thrilling unease of Kinsmead Comp and Mr Dickins's English and drama classes. I did not want to move away from Jess, a girl who had turned out to be a true friend, but, above everything, I did not want to leave JJ.

'What's the matter, precious?' Mums said, pulling me close for a group hug. 'Aren't you over the moon?' The thought crossed my mind that she had secretly planned this all along. Maybe she was so outraged that I was in love with someone from a council estate that she had decided to make up with Grandma Violet just to put distance between JJ and me. I wouldn't put it past her.

'Yes, Mums,' I said feebly.

Great, I thought as I slunk off to my room to be miserable. Now I would need to pray for *two* miracles.

# Chapter 21

Two whole days had passed and there had been no JJ texts, no late-night secret phone calls conducted from underneath my duvet so that Mums wouldn't hear us, not even a lousy email.

I couldn't blame him for giving me the silent treatment. After all, I had been the one to walk away from him, not the other way round. He probably thought I had washed my hands of him. Or maybe he was just giving me time to get my head round everything. But I had hoped he might try to contact me again, try to convince me to see things his way. Deep down, I wanted him to run after me, bombard me with texts and phone calls asking for my understanding, or to say he was sorry he had hurt me. But so far there had been nothing, and nothing, let me tell you, is as bad as nothing.

Since our heated conversation, I had found myself swinging back and forth between intense anger (how could he not contact me? I only wanted to save him from a life behind bars for crying out loud!) and utter self-loathing and despair (how could I have turned my back on him like that?).

It didn't help that Mums had been in a nauseatingly fabulous mood for the last forty-eight hours. Since her little Cotswolds announcement she had not stopped smiling. On top of everything, her fruity cosmetics range was selling like hot cakes down at Portobello Market and people were beginning to place much larger orders. An upmarket cosmetics brand had even shown an interest in stocking her bestselling cucumber eye-bag-busting lotion. Apparently, it had been a real hit with the cool, twenty-four-hour party girls in the area and they simply could not get enough of it.

I stared out of the window at Hamlet Tower. Its brutal concrete façade stared back at me in the cold and unforgiving December greyness. I smiled as I looked at JJ's ode to Piccalilli painted on the railway wall. I thought about all the commuters and tourists who would have seen it as they passed by on the train. It was ironic to think that Piccalilli would remain here when I would be long gone, a piece of history, a monument to mine and JJ's love. I wished I could turn myself into a cartoon, paint myself on Piccalilli's back and stay forever on that wall too.

I heard Mums come up the stairs. She was humming happily to herself.

'Gracie, darling, can I come in?' She entered before I could reply. She was wearing her favourite cream slacks and voluminous Pucci blouse teamed with a matching headscarf and a cashmere cardigan draped over her shoulders. 'I don't want to disturb you if you're busy,' she said, perching herself at the end of my bed and watching me as I sat on the windowsill, staring out into the distance. I wondered if JJ might be at home and if he was looking out of the window and thinking about me.

Mums was silent for a moment. 'What's troubling you, darling?' she asked in unusually soft and kind tones. 'You've seemed awfully distant since I told you about Grandma Violet's.' I dropped the net curtain but didn't turn and face her. 'Gracie . . .'

I finally looked round. 'It's great news,' I said, my lack of enthusiasm alarmingly apparent. 'About Granny V's and the Cotswolds, I mean.'

'Tigs has packed his things already,' Mums laughed, 'and we're not leaving for a week and a half yet! He's terribly excited.' She watched my face carefully. 'We've got a fair bit of packing to do too,' she sighed scanning the room. 'But I'll help, darling, besides, we're dab hands at this packing and unpacking lark now, aren't we?' she smiled. I couldn't bring myself to smile back.

'It's the boy, isn't it?' she said quietly. 'You're sad about leaving JJ.' She had called him by his name, as if finally acknowledging that he existed.

'Yes,' I said, my voice breaking slightly. But sad didn't quite describe how I really felt. Crushed, destroyed, heartbroken, they were much better words. Suddenly I longed to tell her the truth about how I really felt about JJ, about the missing money and the police. I wanted to be able to confide in her, to be open and honest. I felt as though I needed her advice. Although it seemed we were forever holding our feelings back, scared of what the other might think or say, I realised that what we had been through in the last year or so had brought us closer together. I had seen more of her, for one thing. Lack of space in our new/old house had made it impossible for us to avoid each other, which in turn had forced us to become more involved in each other's lives.

'Please don't tell me there's plenty more fish in the aquarium,' I sniffed, predicting some kind of condescending response. 'It may have worked with other boys but it's different with JJ.'

'So I can see,' she said.

I quickly glanced at her.

'The moment I met your father,' she began, 'I knew I would end up marrying him. Don't ask me how. Sixth sense perhaps, or no sense more like,' she snorted a little, 'but I knew. Something inside me just *felt* it.'

'Really?' I said, surprised by her impromptu confession.

'He was so young and charming and terribly eccentric,' she sighed dreamily. 'My mother, your Granny Violet, thought he was quite insane. He used to drive around in this funny little sports car with an open roof – in all weathers – cravat flying behind him, goggles on, like Toad of Toad Hall. I loathed him picking me up in that car. Aside from the fact that all the neighbours would stare, it played absolute merry hell with my hair. Anyway. He was different, your dad. I fell in love with him almost instantly.'

Now I really was shocked. Although I knew Mums loved Dad, I had never, not once, heard her say as much.

She continued. 'At one point, after your father and I had been courting for a couple of months, my daddy thought we might have to move to Hampshire. As you know, he was an officer in the Royal Navy and Mummy and I pretty much had to up sticks and move around the country with him wherever he went. Oh, I cried myself to sleep for three weeks thinking I would have to leave your father. I couldn't eat, I couldn't sleep, I simply couldn't bear the thought of being parted from him.' She closed her eyes as if the pain of the memory was too much. 'Your Granny V was so worried about me that she agreed your father could come and live with us if indeed we did have to move from Richmond. Can you imagine?! Your Grandma Violet actually agreeing to let your father and me live in sin?' Mums chuckled. 'She insisted on separate bedrooms of course!' Mums glanced at me and I felt myself go a little red. 'It never came to that though. Daddy stayed put and so your father and I continued our romance.' She paused for a moment and looked at me, her brown eyes shining. 'So you see, darling, I *do* know how it feels to leave someone behind. Or at least I know the thought of it.' She reached out to me and put her hand on top of mine. It was comforting.

'JJ is in trouble,' I found myself confessing. 'The ticket money for the play was stolen from the youth centre and they think he did it but he didn't, I swear on my life,' I garbled. 'These two boys, the Dulcie twins, they took the money, but JJ won't tell the police this for fear of being treated as a pariah for grassing on people from his estate. It's some kind of ridiculous law among people who live on Hamlet. If you snitch to the police – even if it's the truth – terrible things happen to you and your family, and people put dog mess in your letter box and spit at you in the street and everything.'

I watched her face as it flashed with horror and then sadness.

'Oh, Gracie, that's dreadful,' she said. 'Poor JJ.' This was not quite the reaction I had anticipated. I was expecting stern looks of 'I told you so'.

'So you believe me then?' I said. 'You believe that JJ didn't do it? I mean, I know you think everyone from a council estate is a thief, but really it's not true. JJ is a good person. He would never steal, or lie, despite the image and everything – he's just not like that.'

Everything came out in a rush. I told her about how I had become angry and walked away from him, about how we had not spoken since and how hopeless I felt. Mums put her arm around me and for once it didn't feel awkward or contrived. It felt warm and reassuring, like a soft, familiar blanket. I leaned into her and tucked my head up under her chin like I did as a child.

'Well, I suppose he is nothing if not loyal,' she said. 'Wrong as I think it is. What will he do now?'

'I don't know,' I said, tears beginning to blur my vision. 'I think the police will probably want to speak to me,' I added nervously. 'They will want to know if I know anything.'

'We'll be ready for them,' she said softly.

'I couldn't bear it if they sent him to prison for a crime he didn't commit! What with Dad in prison too . . . ' A rogue tear escaped from my eye and dropped on to the duvet next to me.

'Oh, darling,' Mums said, holding me as I began to cry. 'I couldn't bear it either. I would hate to see you in such pain. I know I haven't approved of this relationship. You must understand it is not because I don't like JJ – far from it, he seems like a very nice young man and he clearly adores you – but I was worried something like this might happen. I am not merely being a frightful snob – he lives by another set of rules to us, Gracie,' she sighed. 'It doesn't make him a bad person, just different.' I nodded as I blew my nose loudly on a tissue. 'Poor JJ,' Mums said again, 'throwing his life away over some silly code of conduct. It's such a waste. So pointless.' She shook her head. 'If there was a way I could help him, I would.'

'Thanks Mums,' I croaked.

'Talk to him. Try to help him. If he loves you, he will listen.'

It felt strange to hear Mums talk about JJ loving me, as if she might believe it could be true. I had already said so much, I decided to go the whole hog and tell her about Dad's letter.

'If only he were here,' she said sadly, 'he would know what to do. This single parent business is rather tricky sometimes.' She smiled warmly and I noticed she had tears in her eyes too.

'You've done a stellar job, Mums,' I said. What's more, I think I meant it.

'You think so?' she said.

'Definitely.' I nodded. 'You can cook now for one thing.' Suddenly, among our tears there was laughter. It had never sounded so good.

# Chapter 22

**M**ums stayed true to her word. Later that day, the police turned up on our doorstep and she calmly invited them through to the kitchen. Despite her stoic façade, I could tell she was nervous because she was doing her manic twisting thing with a button on her Pucci blouse. Cal hovered in the doorway making garrotting gestures behind the police officers' backs. Mums gave him one of her looks and I had to put my hand over my mouth to stop myself from having a fit of nervous giggles.

The taller of the two police officers asked where I was on the night of the theft.

'She was here, with me!' Mums said defensively. 'We watched the second part of that docu-drama on Henry the Eighth's wives, didn't we, Grace?'

'Yes,' I nodded compliantly. It was all true.

'Then our friend, Boris, from next door popped in. He's Russian you know,' Mums said, even though it had absolutely no relevance whatsoever. 'Surely you're not suggesting that Grace had anything to do with this theft, are you?' Mums sounded affronted. She had promised not to tell the police what I had told her about JJ and the Dulcie twins but I was beginning to worry that she might crack under the pressure. 'She would never have been involved in taking that money. If it wasn't for her and the other actors, there would never have been any money there in the first place!'

The female police officer gave Mums an understanding nod before turning to me and saying, 'Grace, do you know a boy by the name of Jay Jones?'

'Yes,' I said, suddenly aware how a simple word like yes can sound incriminating when spoken in front of officers of the law.

'Is he a friend?' the policewoman asked.

'He's her boyfriend,' Cal said helpfully. 'They *luuurve* each other.'

'Yes, thank you, Cal,' Mums said sternly. 'War documentary. History Channel. You'll miss the beginning.' She dismissed him from the kitchen with a flick of her hand.

'He is my boyfriend, yes.' I said.

'Can you tell us when you last saw him?'

'He didn't do it,' I blurted out. 'JJ would never have taken the money. He wanted to help raise that money for the community just as much as anyone else. And that's not his tag either – the picture of the dove in the boys' toilets. It was someone else's attempt at copying him.'

I heard a ping as the button from Mums's blouse fell to the floor. I had said too much already. Then, just as things seemed to be going from bad to worse, there was another knock on the door. It was Boris. He had seen the police car outside and dropped by to see if all was well. Cal led him through to the kitchen.

'They're interrogating Grace,' he said, adding, 'they have ways of making you talk!'

'I was worried,' Boris said, greeting Mums in his thick Russian accent. 'Is everything all right?'

Mums briefly explained the situation to Boris, about the missing money and JJ's arrest.

'But this cannot be so,' Boris said, turning to the police officers. 'I am seeing *two* boys coming out of the youth centre at nine o'clock on this night. I am checking my watch because I am rushing home to catch a film about the Russian Revolution on Channel Four. I am thinking the boys looking suspicious. They are also looking the same as each other! Yes, I remember.' Boris was nodding frantically. 'I not see the boy JJ,' he said, pointing at me. 'He is Miss Grace's friend. A nice boy.'

'Are you sure Mr . . . er, Mr . . . '

'Sergeyev, Boris Sergeyev. And yes, I am one hundred per cent sure that I am seeing two boys running from the youth centre. Two boys that look like each other.'

And would you believe it, just like that, a fairy godmother, a hairy, fairy godfather, saved the day.

I couldn't wait to call JJ and tell him about Boris's statement to the police. Surely this would put them on the right path and take the heat off JJ? Boris was an eye witness after all and had seen the Dulcie twins running from the scene of the crime. I knew JJ was not yet off the hook but it felt like only a matter of time.

'You are so not going to believe everything that has happened here today,' I blurted out to JJ on the phone, excitedly forgetting that we were not supposed to be talking and that I was supposed to be angry with him.

'The police came round asking questions and Mums was brilliant, and then they asked me if I knew you and of course I said yes, and Cal told them that you were my boyfriend, and I didn't deny it, and then, you wouldn't believe it, but Boris – the Russian from next door – turns up and hears what's been going on, and suddenly from nowhere says that he saw two boys who looked alike running from the scene of the crime, and that it wasn't you he saw and that you're a really nice person and everything, and now he's down at the station giving a statement, so they're bound to find out that it was the Dulcie twins who took the money and you'll be off the hook and they'll have to apologise to you for wrongful arrest, at least, I hope they'll apologise to you because they should and everything and . . .'

'Grace!' JJ said as I continued to blather on excitedly. 'Grace! You're freaking me out. What are you talking about?'

'The Russian,' I said, as if that should be explanation enough. 'He's put the Dulcie twins at the scene of the crime. You're saved!' I squealed. 'We must celebrate. Please forgive me for not speaking to you. It's just that I've had such mixed feelings about all this and I just couldn't bear to think . . .'

'Whoa! Slow down there, lady!' he said. 'The police have already dropped the charges, they've just been round to see me this minute. Some new evidence has come to light. Turns out the Dulcies' dabs were all over the cash box where the money was kept and they found their DNA in the toilets where they broke in. I'm off the hook!'

'Oh God!' I said, feeling a little silly. 'That's fantastic! Come on, let's go for an all-you-can-eat Chinese buffet celebration at Mr Chong's on the high street – my treat!'

JJ was quiet for a moment. 'You're not still angry with me then?' he asked tentatively. 'You're not going to start poking me with your chopsticks or anything are you?'

'There's only one way to find out!' I said.

Although I was ecstatic about the truth coming to light, I still couldn't help thinking about the fact that JJ had been so prepared to do time for a crime he did not commit. I watched him as he tried to scoop up a slippery mushroom with his chopsticks.

'This is top scran, this,' he said between mouthfuls of greasy noodle. 'Thanks for offering to take me out. I promise it'll be my turn next time. If I make enough dosh I'll even take you up west somewhere posh, like one of them steakhouses or somewhere. We'll have prawn cocktails and big fat steaks and gateaux for afters – the works,' he said.

I smiled. His 'next time' speeches always touched me. I knew he meant them, every word, even if they were unlikely to happen.

'How does it feel to be a free man?' I asked, unable to stop smiling.

'Stuff it,' JJ said as the mushroom once again slipped from his chopsticks. He picked up a fork and stabbed the offending vegetable gleefully before putting it in his mouth. 'It feels like the best day of my life,' he said, chewing. 'Next to the day I met you, of course!'

'Smoothie!' I replied. 'What will happen to the Dulcie Twins now?' I asked. 'Will they be arrested?'

'I guess so,' JJ shrugged. 'Not too bothered to tell you the truth. They'll get what's coming to them. I'm just glad it's all over.'

'Me too,' I said, looking at him. 'Jay, there's something . . .'

'If you're about to start telling me off again then I just have to say this,' he interrupted. 'Over the last few days I've done nothing but sit and think and think and sit and I've decided that you were right all along. It was mental to think that I would be prepared to go to prison for a crime I didn't do, just to save face.'

I looked down at my bowl of pink prawn noodles. How was I going to break it to him that we were leaving?

'I know why you were angry,' he said, putting his fork down for a moment and taking hold of my hand candidly. 'I'd have felt the same if it had been the other way round. It made me realise how much you care.'

'Oh Jay,' I said, wishing I had the guts to clear the table with one swoop of my arm like they do in films and climb over it to kiss him.

'Everything that's happened,' he said, 'it's made me realise how much I want to get away. Leave Hamlet Tower and go; go anywhere, find a place of my own. A place where there are no stupid rules. A place that's safe for you to come and visit me without worrying about getting mugged on the way home, where we can get cosy together and not be disturbed.' JJ paused for a second. 'I've been down the dole office today. There's a firm in Paddington, they're looking for an office junior. You know, someone to do all the crap and make the tea and stuff. I've probably got more chance of winning the lottery than I have of getting an interview, but I've decided I'm going to go for it anyway. What have I got to lose?' He paused for a second. 'I've been wasting time, Grace,' he said earnestly, 'dreaming about being some great street artist who's going to take over the world. I know it isn't ever going to happen. It was all just a fantasy, a pipe dream. I've realised if I want to make it in this world, I need to start getting real. It's time I grew up. I want to look after you, Grace,' he said, playing with the little flower ring on my finger. 'I want to be able to take you out for nice meals and buy you presents like a proper boyfriend. I want to get a car and go for days out down the coast. I'm eighteen years old in less than two months and soon you'll be seventeen. We're not kids any more.'

'But you can't give up on your dreams!' I protested. 'Your art is your life. It's who you are. You can't throw away all your hopes and ambitions to work in some dingy office somewhere. You'll hate it.'

He looked at me with a mixture of warmth and sadness. 'Maybe,' he said, taking another forkful of chow mein. My appetite had suddenly abandoned me.

'Please don't think you need to do any of this for me,' I said, pushing the bowl away. 'I have every faith in you, in your talent. I don't care if you're as poor as a church mouse. I love you just the way you are.'

I linked my fingers in his and felt sick inside. He was making plans, looking to the future, a future he wanted to share with me. It was all so unfair, just when things had finally come right. I wished I could forget all about the Cotswolds, erase it from my mind. I just wanted to sit there in the moment, sucking up Chinese noodles from a plastic bowl and drinking Diet Cokes as we discussed the rest of our lives together.

'Jay,' I said quietly. 'We're leaving.'

Jay looked up, perplexed. 'Why?' he said. 'Don't you like the food? I know it's probably full of MSG and additives and stuff but . . .'

'No, I mean we're leaving the area. Moving away, moving home.'

JJ's fork made an angry clattering sound as it hit the bowl. 'No,' he said shaking his head. 'No!'

'We're going to live with my Grandma Violet in the Cotswolds. Mums has set it all up. We leave in ten days.'

'Ten days!' The chair made a horrible screeching sound as JJ stood up from the table, his eyes wide with horror. He put his hands up to his head. 'Tell me this is not really happening,' he said. 'I'm in a nightmare, right? Just pinch me!' He held his arm out towards me. 'You can't leave. I won't let you,' he said defiantly. 'You can come and live with my family until we get a place of our own. I'll square it with Ma. It'll be a squeeze but we'll manage.'

The people on the next table were beginning to look over at us. I finally managed to look up at him and I saw his eyes were all watery. I burst into tears.

'Is everything OK?' the waitress asked as she came over to take our empty glasses. 'Food's not that bad, huh?' She raised a concerned eyebrow.

JJ flashed her a thin smile. 'We're just leaving,' he said.

# Chapter 23

**O**ur footsteps were the only sound as we walked solemnly along the canal bank home. I wondered if this might be the last time we would ever make this journey together. The thought of it sent ripples of anguish through my chest, a thousand tiny needles stabbing at my heart. A sense of helplessness overwhelmed me. Would I ever be in control of my own destiny? Would there come a day when I would be able to make my own decisions on where I would live and with whom? Now that I had met JJ, all I wanted was to stay. They say home is where your heart is and my heart was right there, with him.

'I'm sorry I ruined the night,' I said, breaking the stony silence between us. 'We were supposed to be celebrating . . .'

He shook his head. 'I'm glad you told me. If we've only got ten days left to be together then I don't want to waste a single second of it.' His voice was soft, almost fragile.

I blinked back tears.

'Listen, what I said, about you coming to live with me at Ma's. I mean it you know. Ma won't mind and the twins already love you. You can be part of the family.'

I brushed a tear away as it silently fell from my cheek.

'Oh Jay,' I said. 'There's seven of you already in that tiny flat. There's no room.'

'We'll *make* room,' he said, determined. 'Please, Grace, at least think about it.'

'I'd live in a cardboard box with you,' I said, 'but Mums would never allow it.' A hard lump stuck in my throat as I swallowed. He knew I was right.

'But I don't think I can stand being without you.' He stopped and turned to me. I looked up into his eyes. 'All this,' he said, gesturing around him, 'I can't make it without you, Grace. You've made my life round here bearable.'

'Please don't say that,' I said, my voice cracking. 'We'll still be able to see each other. You can come and stay. Stay for whole summers,' I said, my enthusiasm hollow. 'The Cotswolds, it's not a million miles away . . .' But we both knew it might as well be.

'I knew this would happen,' JJ said, almost angry. 'From the moment I met you, I knew that one day you would go away again and I would lose you.'

My coat flapped open with a sudden gust of wind but I didn't bother wrapping it around me. I let the cold bite against my body, anything to take my mind away from the torment I felt raging through me.

My mind turned back to my conversation with Mums and how she felt at the thought of being separated from Dad. What had she said? 'If there's any way I can help JJ . . .'

'Perhaps Mums will let you come and live with us!' I said, my thoughts spilling out loud. 'There would be room. Granny V's cottage, well, it's more of a house than a cottage, it has four bedrooms. Yes!' I said, wondering why I hadn't thought of it sooner. 'You can come and be part of *our* family!'

JJ glanced at me sideways from the corner of his eye. 'Your mum will never go for it,' he said, though there was a flicker of hope in his voice. 'She's only just about come to terms with the fact that you and I are an item.'

'Wouldn't it be wonderful?' I said excitely. 'We could go for long walks in the countryside and have picnics in the meadows. You could find a job or help Mums with her new business perhaps. We could spend all our time together, somewhere beautiful, away from here, away from Hamlet and all its problems and stupid codes of conduct.' I was already getting far too carried away.

'Please don't,' he said. 'It's bad enough as it is but, saying all this and giving me hope, it's just torture.'

'All is not lost,' I said with renewed energy. 'You leave Mums to me.'

'You are *so* not going to leave here. I won't allow it, *Uh-uh*.' Jess was standing up in her bedroom, dressed in stripy pyjamas with her hand on her hip defiantly. 'If this is a joke . . .'

'It's not, really.' I said, miserably. It was early Thursday morning. I had been putting off telling Jess till now, knowing how hard it would be, and wanting to tell her face to face, not on the phone.

Jess fell down next to me on the bed. 'But you *can't* leave,' she said. 'I'll go back to being the posh bird again.'

I managed a small smile. 'You'll cope,' I said.

Jess stared at me. 'What will I do?' she said. 'What will *JJ* do without you? This is a disaster. This is not how it ends in *Grease!*' she spluttered. 'They make off into the sunset together in that flying car thingy. No, no, no. This is all wrong.' Automatically, Jess stuffed her hand into a bag of cheesy Wotsits perched on her bedside cabinet and crammed a handful into her mouth nervously. 'This is your mum's idea, right?'

'Who else's?' I snorted.

'Bloody parents,' she said. 'Seriously, Grace, you can't leave me now, not when things are just starting to get interesting between me and Zone.'

'Sid,' I giggled.

'*Sid* is actually rather lovely,' Jess sighed. 'If you go, our cosy foursome will be destroyed.'

'Well, I'm sorry to ruin your plans.' I turned to her, more seriously. 'I'll really miss you, Jess,' I said, taking her hand. 'You've been such a great friend to me since I came here. I don't know what I would've done without you.' I quickly looked down at the carpet to avoid eye contact. I'd cried enough these last few days.

'Got your head kicked in for one thing,' Jess said in that spiky way I had grown to love. She snuggled closer to me on the bed. 'I'm really going to miss you too,' she said. 'You're a mate. Without you putting in a good word for me, I reckon it would have been another year before me and Zone ever got it on.' She giggled.

I suspected that, given more time together, my friendship with Jess could've gone from strength to strength. Perhaps we could've become as close as Tave and I once were. Now I would never know.

'You'll come and stay, won't you?' I asked, wondering if history might repeat itself and she would forget me as soon as I was out of sight, just as Tave had done. 'We can spend summers together. Maybe you can bring Sid, sorry, Zone with you and . . .' A hard lump in my throat prevented me from continuing.

'Of course,' she smiled, her eyes a little glassy, 'you can bet yer bazookas I will!' And we both laughed to stop ourselves from crying as we hugged each other tightly.

Mums was sticking labels on boxes when I returned home from Jess's. She had started packing with fevered enthusiasm. I wondered how it would be best to broach the subject of JJ coming to live with us. Although our recent conversation had made me feel closer to her, it was not enough to stop my nerves jangling.

'You know I'll almost be sad to leave in a way,' she said as I sat down at the kitchen table watching her carefully bubble-wrap the good china. 'It's as if living here has united us all in a funny sort of way. Still, it will be wonderful to be in the clean air again, away from all the pollution and the noise, don't you think, darling?'

'I suppose,' I said, as I began psyching myself up for the big Q. 'But it really would be wonderful if JJ was coming with us,' I said carefully, scared of it sounding too much like a question.

'You'll need to start packing your room soon, kitten,' she replied, without even acknowledging what I had just said. 'The removal men are coming first thing a week on

Saturday and I don't want you leaving it all to the last minute as usual.'

'I'll start tonight,' I promised. 'Anyway, I'm a dab hand these days.'

Mums glanced at me to see if I was being sarcastic or not.

'Mums . . . ' I said, nervously pressing a piece of bubble-wrap between my fingers. It made a satisfying pop.

'Yes, darling.'

'Why did Dad do what he did?' It was not the question I had planned but somehow it felt like the right time to ask it.

Mums stopped wrapping for a second and took a sharp intake of breath. We both knew the time had come for the truth. Placing her Wedgwood vase carefully down on the table, she pulled up a rickety chair and sat down.

'The root of all tragedy,' Mums sighed.

'Root of all tragedy?'

'Money, darling. We had money troubles . . . though I knew nothing of it at the time,' she said, her voice trailing off thoughtfully. 'You see, your father held the purse strings. He earned the money and I, well, I just spent it.' She raised her eyebrows with what looked like regret. 'I always assumed he would tell me if things became difficult. The antiques business was losing money and we had such huge overheads. Our lifestyle, Embers and its upkeep, the gardens and the staff, the cars and the schools and the pool and the pony – it was draining money we didn't really have. She sighed again. 'Anyway, when your father happened to meet someone who made him an interesting offer, he saw a way out of the hole we were in and took it.' Mums absent-mindedly rubbed her hands down the front of her slacks, wiping off invisible dirt. 'Problem was, the offer was not legitimate. But your father is a proud man, Grace. He couldn't bear the thought of us having to cut back and change our lives, stop your education and my spending sprees. He just wanted everything to be tickety-boo. He hated change.'

I watched as the frown lines furrowed deeper into my mother's brow. I felt as though I should comfort her but wanted her to continue, so I held back.

'But he was wrong,' she said sadly. 'He thought he could make a bit of money in the short term to get us out of a tricky spot. By the time he realised exactly what he had got himself involved in, it was all far too late and there was no way back. He was trapped. Oh, the judge said it was greed,' Mums said dismissively, 'but it wasn't greed. It was *need*. It was the need to keep his family in the life they knew and loved that made him do what he did. I've always said he did it for us. I know his crimes were wrong, but he will always be a hero in my eyes. However much I let him down.'

'Let him down?' I said. 'How did you let him down?'

'Oh, come on, Gracie. I must've been a terrible wife. He couldn't even tell me when things were desperate,' she snorted. 'I remember we once watched this TV documentary about men who had lost their jobs and spent years pretending to their wives they were still going to work. They would get up in the morning and put on a shirt and tie and off they went to 'work' when really they were spending all day in some grotty café drinking endless cups of coffee and worrying themselves into an early heart attack about the bills. I'd said to your father, "Nothing like that would ever happen to us because we have no secrets, do we, Edgar? Besides, I'm not that much of an ogre, surely?" And he turned to me and said, "Penelope, you really do say the most ridiculous things at times!"' She laughed sadly at the memory. 'When it came down to it, even after all those years of marriage, he still couldn't tell me when he was in trouble. He was too ashamed.'

Mums quickly wiped her eyes with the back of her sleeve. I reached out and touched her hand lightly. I had never heard her so unguarded.

'Anyway, darling,' she said, composing herself. 'It's in the past now. Your father paid the highest price he could for his crimes – he lost everything: his liberty, his businesses, his reputation and his family, albeit only temporarily. But soon he will be home with us and we can start again. Lessons learned – all of us.'

I stared at her. She had such an innate elegance, even when packing boxes and crying about the past. I realised that she was quite beautiful on the inside too, kind and forgiving, loving and hopeful. Suddenly she felt like a friend as well as my mum.

'I don't blame you for being angry with him,' she said, watching my hand as it lightly rested on top of hers. 'The more we love someone, sometimes the harder it is to forgive them.'

In a peculiar way I found myself feeling almost glad

about everything that had happened. Now it seemed we were closer than we'd ever been before.

'I love you, Mums,' I found myself saying for the first time since I could remember.

She stood up and came towards me, putting her arms around me. 'Oh Gracie, my beautiful darling Gracie,' she said, as she pulled me into her soft, sweet-smelling neck. 'I love you so much too.'

Together we stood, in that small, dank kitchen, where Mums had learned to cook proper food and we had sat and laughed and cried in equal measures during the past four months, and we held on to each other tightly. We had come through a war together. We were scratched and we were bruised, but we had fought on to see another day, a better day.

'So,' she said when I finally unstuck my tear-sodden face from her warm chest, 'are you going to waste time getting all sentimental on your old Mums here, or are you going to run and find that boyfriend of yours and ask him if he wants a new home in the Cotswolds, hmm?'

It was a question she would never have to ask twice.

# Chapter 24

The dictionary says that happiness is 'the quality of being happy. Good fortune; pleasure; contentment; joy'. But I felt something more than all of those words put together as I calmly strolled through Sometime Place. I needed a new word – something bigger, more flamboyant, something colourful and rich and all-consuming. 'Happiness' just didn't cut it. I texted JJ:

*Meet me at the entrance to Hamlet in half an hour.*
*Got some news. Love G x*

I had not given anything away in the message. I wanted to feel the full benefit of telling him face to face. The anticipation of his reaction sent tingles all through my body.

I didn't rush to Hamlet estate. Suddenly it felt as though I had all the time in the world. Despite the low, bright winter sunshine that made me squint, it was still somewhat chilly and JJ, sporting a battered leather bomber jacket, stripy scarf and baggy jeans worn low on his hips, was not dressed for such a cold day. He looked gorgeous though. All ruffled in that scruffily sexy way of his. Luckily, I had news that I knew would warm him from the inside out.

'The Cotwolds. With you. Your mum has said that I can come and *live* in the Cotswolds *with you?*' JJ was repeating my words back to me as if I must be mistaken. I sensed I might need to repeat myself a few times before it sank in.

I nodded. 'Yes,' I said, my measured tones belying the excitement within. 'With us. With me. In our Granny V's cottage. You'll have your own room and everything!' The tips of my fingers touched his, making the hair on the back of my neck stand up.

'I've never had my own room before,' JJ said, his eyes wide with a mixture of excitement and disbelief. 'I . . . I want to believe it,' he stammered. 'I mean, she definitely . . . she really said yes?'

'Yes!' I screamed. 'YES, YES, YES! We're going to be together. We're going to *live* in a beautiful place somewhere far, far from here *together* and life is going to be just so amazing. I'll teach you how to ride a horse,' I blathered, 'and clay pigeon shoot in the woods – it's really good fun – and we can go mushroom picking and fishing with Cal and swimming in the lake . . . and . . . and Mums said you can earn a bit of keep by helping out in the garden and round the house. She doesn't want you to think that this is charity or anything.' I stopped my rambling to be serious for a moment. 'She knows we're in love, JJ. She understands. We talked more than we've ever done before, about Dad and you and me – everything!' I said, looking deep into his eyes. 'Just think: no more Hamlet estate; no more cramped living or noise or pollution, no gangs or codes and stupid laws. We'll be free. Happy and free. Together forever. Just like we said.'

222

'Seems like you got everything sorted,' he said, his dimple made more pronounced by his broad smile. Our lips met, their warmth melting the crisp air around us. 'Please say you'll come,' I breathed into him.

He stepped back from me a little, his soft, strong hands gripping my shoulders. 'You really need me to answer that?'

I wrapped my arms around him and he did the same. We stood together in the middle of Sometime Place, embracing like the lovers in Rodin's statue of 'The Kiss', the closeness of our bodies keeping us warm in the bitter breeze.

'I'll have to talk to Ma,' he said. 'She'll be made up. She's always wanted something better for me and now . . . well, this is my chance, Grace.' His warm breath gently tickled the nape of my neck as he spoke. 'The Cotswolds . . . ' he said, playing with the word as if it were a new and exciting toy. 'I can't believe it.'

I nestled into his chest and smiled uncontrollably. Truth was, I couldn't believe it either.

We had so little time and so much to do. Firstly, JJ would need to talk to his mum, and tell her the news. Mums had even agreed to meet Mary to discuss everything. After all, JJ was her eldest son, and she would need to know that he would be well looked after. Cal was ecstatic about the news too. 'It'll be like having the brother I've always wanted. Not that having a sister isn't cool,' he added, not wanting to hurt my feelings. I laughed. Nothing anyone could say or do could knock me off my cloud right now. 'We'll be able to play war games in the woods, and Dungeons and Dragons! It'll be ace,' Cal said, his eyes wide with the possibilities.

'I know, Tigs,' I replied, digging him playfully in the ribs. 'Maybe I'll get a moment's peace!'

I smiled secretly to myself. My story, it seemed, was about to have a happy ending.

JJ was helping me put my old CDs and DVDs into boxes as I packed up my room. '*Gone With The Wind* ... *Wuthering Heights*...*Casablanca*? Never heard of them!' He pulled a face. 'Are they chick-flicks?'

I giggled. '*Classic* chick-flicks. You'd love them, being the softy you are underneath.'

He shot me an unconvinced look. 'And what's this?' He pulled out The Rebekahs' 'Obsession' CD from my collection. 'Wow. Now that we're going to be living together, I hope that doesn't mean you'll always have the first say in what goes on the stereo or the telly!'

'Hey,' I said, grabbing an old soft Snoopy toy from one of the boxes and throwing it at him, 'don't be so cheeky! Anyway, it's better than all that samey hip hop stuff you play – yo, yo, yo and errr, yo!' I burst into a fit of giggles.

He lunged forward and playfully wrestled me to my bedroom floor. 'Can you really believe this is happening?' he panted as he rolled on top of me. 'You and me, going to live in the Cotswolds together like some old married couple?'

'Less of the old,' I said, pushing him off me. I sat up and straightened my ruffled hair. 'Your mum's definitely OK with it, then?'

'Yeah,' JJ said, bringing his knees up to his chest and wrapping his arms across them. He absent-mindedly looked at the floor. 'She can't believe some posh family wants to take me in as one of their own. It's a chance, you know, to have a decent life.' He shrugged. 'She's sad about me going but she wants me to be happy. For us to be happy. She knows this is an opportunity of a lifetime.'

I picked up my old Snoopy and stared at his battered, careworn ears. 'You'll still be able to paint,' I said, sensing a little sadness from JJ. 'I'm sure there are facilities in the Cotswolds.'

He broke my gaze. 'Anyway, how come girls have so much more stuff than boys? You've only been here a few months and look at all this!' He picked up a handful of my paraphernalia, CDs and books and old photos . . .

'Get used to it,' I said with a huge grin.

The following days passed in a blur of boxes and brown tape as I packed up my life once more. Only this time, my heart did not feel heavy as I wrapped my possessions in old newspaper. There was only fevered anticipation at the thought of what the future might bring.

It was Friday evening before I knew it, the night before we were due to leave for Granny V's, and I had accompanied JJ back to the estate for a few last-minute checks.

We walked hand in hand along Goldborne Road, past the smelly fishmonger's and our favourite café. JJ seemed a little quieter than usual.

'Christmas is going to be wicked,' I enthused. 'We'll

have a huge tree with squillions of decorations and everything. Granny V's Christmas lunches are legendary. She cooks the most enormous turkey; it can barely fit in the Aga!'

'What's an Aga?' JJ asked.

'Oh, it's a big oven type thingy. It's great. They can heat your whole house!'

'Oh,' JJ said as he continued to stare ahead of him. He sounded a little flat. 'And once we've had the great big feast, we open our presents by the tree. Sometimes we roast chestnuts over Granny V's little wood fire, just for effect mainly because actually I think chestnuts taste awful.'

'You open your presents *after* dinner?' JJ asked.

'Yes. We take turns. One by one. It's fun.' I assured him. 'Why, do you do it differently in your family?' I asked.

'The twins are up at five, ripping open everything in sight like a couple of wild animals,' JJ smiled affection- ately. 'There's always paper everywhere. I usually spend the morning with them, playing with their new toys. Then I go back to bed for a couple of hours and then help Ma do dinner. When the twins were a bit smaller, Ma used to save up all year for their Christmas toys, and they always ended up playing with the boxes and wrapping paper more than the actual presents! That always made me laugh . . . ' His voice trailed off into the distance. 'You know I don't have presents for everyone,' he suddenly said, concerned. 'I've just about managed to buy my own family a little something each.'

'Don't be silly,' I said. 'No one expects you to buy

them a present. The fact that you'll be there with us – that we'll all be together is the best present in the entire world.' I squeezed JJ's hand hopefully.

'Yeah,' he said. 'The best present anyone could ever want.'

We plodded on in silence, the noise of Goldborne Road throbbing around us, and a slight sense of unease crept up on me as we strolled, our arms swinging in unison as dusk turned into night.

'SURPRISE!'

Greeted by a sea of happy faces, we entered JJ's flat. Everyone was there: JJ's mum, his brothers and sisters, Zone, Trucker, Ultimatum and a few more of his graffiti pals, Jess, Shelly Dacre, a couple more girls from school, some familiar faces from the estate whose names I didn't know, and even Janice Brady, flanked by her hard-faced friends. A banner, homemade from bits of coloured tissue paper, read *GOOD LUCK JJ. WE LOVE U.*

'The twins spent all day making it,' said Mary proudly. 'Didn't you, girls?'

The twins nodded in that eerie, twinny way of theirs. They looked a little sad. There was party food on the small table: cheese and pineapple chunks on sticks, mini sausages and curly crisps, rice-crispy cakes with cherries on the top and egg sandwiches with the crusts cut off.

'To my best boy,' Mary said, raising her mug. 'To JJ.'

'To JJ,' the crowd repeated.

'And to Grace. To JJ and Grace,' Mary added, the tears rolling down her face. JJ went over and hugged his mum.

She suddenly looked small and old in his arms. It brought a lump to my throat. Everyone began tucking into the little spread, laughing and chatting. I stepped back and watched as JJ started talking to his friends. People were putting their arms around him and hugging him. He was smiling and hugging them back. He looked happy so I left him for a moment and went over to Jess, who was standing next to Zone.

'Hey,' she said, putting her arm around me. 'Are you OK? You look a little upset.'

She'd always been able to read my thoughts. I wondered if she was terribly perceptive or if I was just transparent. 'I'm fine,' I lied. I didn't really know why I suddenly felt so upset. I guessed seeing JJ there with all his friends and family . . .

'I can't believe he's going,' Zone said, shaking his head. 'Don't get me wrong. I'm chuffed for him. I mean, he gets to be with you and live in a big house and that.'

'It's really not very big at all,' I said, apologetically.

'It's just never going to be the same without him. We've been friends for so long . . .' Zone looked over at JJ. He was talking to a boy from the estate. I noticed Janice Brady lingering in the background – she had not even looked at me. 'I'm going to miss the old git so much,' Zone finished sadly.

Jess put her arm round him and gave him a squeeze. 'We'll be able to spend summers down there, the four of us. Imagine it, the countryside! All that rolling in the hay and carrot crunching!' said Jess, trying to lighten the moment.

Marianne, JJ's sister, approached us. She gave me a little

hug. 'You will look after him, won't you?' she said as she took my hands in hers earnestly. She was so unbelievably grown-up for her age.

'Of course,' I said, trying to reassure her.

'Ma is beside herself that he's leaving,' she said gently. There was no resentment in her voice, just a terrible wrenching heartbreak that brought back that hard lump to my throat. 'We all are. JJ has been our rock. The man of the house since Dad went.' Her large blue eyes were glassy with tears. 'He's so precious to us – to everyone – we'll miss him so much.'

Unable to speak for fear of crying, I nodded gently so as not to dislodge any of the tears that had formed in my eyes.

'I promise to take very good care of him,' I croaked as she fell into me and hugged me tightly.

JJ was chatting to Janice Brady when I next looked over. It was hardly a big room so I managed to catch little broken snippets of the conversation.

JJ: 'We'll see . . . yes six month trial period . . . always come home . . . love her so much . . . graffing . . . try and do better . . . miss everyone . . . '

Janice: 'You must be mental . . . Ma needs you . . . twins . . . your life is art . . . too different . . . ideas above your station . . . end in tears . . . '

It sounded like Janice was deliberately trying to put doubts in JJ's head. I was livid. I wanted to go over and finally tell her what I thought of her, tell her to get her sticky, chavvy beak out of our business and get a life. She had always hated me. Just because I came from a different place and my face didn't fit, because I didn't speak with a London accent, smoke, drink and swear like she did. If she had only given me a chance then perhaps we could've even been friends.

Jess caught the look of disdain on my face as I stared in Janice's direction.

'Don't let her bother you,' she said, glancing over her shoulder. 'After all, who's had the last laugh? Come on, let's have one of those egg sarnies. I don't know about you but I'm so hungry I could eat a toenail pasty!'

I stayed in the background for the rest of the evening and left JJ to reminisce and say his goodbyes. At one point he looked over at me and mouthed the words, 'Are you OK?' I smiled brightly – perhaps a little too brightly – and mouthed back, 'I'm fine,' and he blew me a kiss, which I pretended to catch.

Soon it was getting late and we had an early start in the morning. The removal men were coming for eight a.m. and we had arranged to pick JJ up at nine.

'I think I'll head off,' I said to him as we crossed paths in the tiny kitchenette.

'You're going?' he said, surprised. 'But this is our little send off. You can't leave already.'

'You stay,' I smiled, touching his arm affectionately. 'They're here for you, really.'

JJ shuffled his feet.

'I'll see you in the morning. Nine o'clock,' I said. 'I'll ring the bell.' I leaned in to kiss him and he pulled me into his arms. He held me tightly and with an urgency that should have made me feel happy but made me anxious.

# The Wrong Boy

'See you at nine,' he said. 'I love you, Grace.'
'I love you too,' I replied. 'Enjoy the rest of the party.'
I slipped away quietly. I was all done with goodbyes.

# Chapter 26

The removal men arrived on time.

'All boxes marked *X* contain breakable goods,' Mums barked at them as they hurriedly marched in and out of 146 Erwine Street like a tribe of ants.

'Careful!' she snapped as she watched a man in a brown coat struggle with two boxes, one on top of the other. 'We've hardly got anything of value left so I don't want you breaking what precious little we do have.'

The men all but ignored her. 'Yes madam, don't worry,' said a man in a cap who looked like the boss. 'My boys have done this before you know.'

I rubbed my sleepy eyes and put my arm around Cal as we stood back and watched, still both in our pyjamas.

'Are you glad to be going?' I yawned at him.

'I suppose. Yes. No. A bit of both actually,' he replied. 'One the one hand, I'll not miss the noise and the stink and my crappy bedroom and on the other . . . well, it's not such a terrible place really, when you think of it. I even liked school in the end.'

The mention of school suddenly made me think of Mr Dickins. I felt a little regret at not having had the chance to say goodbye to him. He had been something of an inspiration to me. I made a mental note to write to him when we got to Granny V's cottage.

'Chop chop,' Mums said as she hurried past Cal and me. 'I'm off to say toodles to Boris next door and I want you both out of those jim-jams by the time I'm back. We'll be leaving soon and have yet to get JJ.'

Getting dressed, I took a good look around my box-room bedroom for the last time. The spiteful crack that ran the length of the wall somehow appeared much less menacing now. I had grown used to it. The shade-less light bulb hung, still, slightly left of centre on the low ceiling. The room was empty once again. I peered out of the window and down at the railway tracks. I remembered the time I had got a little too close to them and how JJ had held me back and kept me safe from the speeding trains. Then, of course, there was my beautiful Piccalilli in all his galloping glory, nostrils flared and snorting. It felt odd to think that, even after I had gone, he would still be there, running free on a grimy London wall.

I stared at Piccalilli for the longest time before finally looking up at the Tower. There it stood, Hamlet Tower, in all its decaying splendour. Looking at it now, I felt that there *was* a certain beauty to it, in the people who lived there, their hopes and dreams. I thought I would miss it in a peculiar sort of way.

The van pulled up outside the front of Hamlet Tower.

'Good Lord,' Mums said under her breath as a bunch of rough-looking kids immediately began circling the van. 'Those van doors had better be locked, driver,' she called out.

'Hurry up, Grace,' she said, impatiently. 'I imagine it's

going to take a while for JJ to get everything down in that lift.' Mums pulled a face as if she had a bad smell under her nose. 'Let's try and be as quick as we can, OK kitten?'

The stinky lift was in good working order as two of the removal men and I went up in it. I figured we would only need to make a couple of journeys at most. It wasn't as if JJ had much to show for his almost seventeen years, just a few paintings and clothes and the usual CDs and DVDs and stuff. I rang the bell. No one answered. I figured the TV was probably on or JJ was busy in his room and hadn't heard us. I rang again. After a few moments, Mary answered the door. She looked pale and drawn as if she had been awake all night. My heart started racing, fuelled by a sudden rush of adrenalin. Had something happened?

'Is everything OK, Mrs Jone–... Mary?' I said. 'Is JJ ready?'

The removal men shuffled uncomfortably behind me.

'Listen, my darling,' she said, taking my hand and holding it tightly. Now she was really was scaring me. 'I can't find the boy anywhere, so I can't.' She glanced at the removal men and pulled me into their hallway, half closing the door for privacy. 'His bags are packed and everything,' she said, looking worried and perplexed, 'but he's nowhere to be found. His brothers have been out looking for him for the last hour, so they have, and I've tried his mobile a million times but it's just going to answer machine. Oh love, I don't know what to say, so I don't.'

Panic and confusion came at me like a freight train and my legs felt too heavy to be able to dodge it. 'Perhaps he's gone to say goodbye to a friend,' I said hopefully. 'Or to the shop to pick up some snacks for the journey . . . '

Mary looked at me and nodded, her anxious smile betraying her true thoughts. 'Aye,' she said soothingly, 'it'll be something like that, I'm sure. Do you want to come in and wait? I'll make you a nice brew. You'll probably not have enough time to drink it before he's back.'

I looked behind me at the removal men. 'If you could give us ten minutes,' I said, shakily. 'I'll need to call Mums.'

'Out? Out where? Oh, for heaven's sake, Gracie, this is really not on,' Mums sighed. 'We're all ready to go down here. Have you tried calling? OK, well, fifteen minutes maximum and then we're off.'

I sat on the threadbare sofa, my heart pounding like an angry caged animal in my chest. I stared at the remnants of last night's farewell send off as Mary made tea in the kitchenette. The twins' banner had come unstuck from above the fireplace and lost some of its tissue paper letters. It now read *G OD LU K J WE LO E U* as it clung desperately to the wall.

'Don't worry about the tea!' I called out to Mary in the kitchen, as I shut the front door behind me.

Mums poked her head out of the car as I sprinted past. 'Grace!' I heard her call out to me. 'For goodness' sakes, what the devil is going on, GRACE?'

I ignored her and carried on running until I reached Sometime Place. It was cold and had started to rain a little, but I hardly noticed as I manically scanned the pardon in search of JJ.

He was sitting on the bench by the tropical plants behind the skate park – our bench. His BMX bike propped up against it, he was dragging heavily on a roll up and clutching something to his chest. He was staring into space as I approached, out of breath, my hair beginning to mat from the increasing rainfall. I sat down next to him, my heart so heavy it felt like a dam about to burst. I waited.

'I can't go with you,' JJ said quietly after a few moments that felt like years. 'I'm so sorry, Grace.' Grey smoke escaped from his mouth as he bit his top lip. I held my breath. My worst fears had been confirmed. 'I spent the whole of last night – all night – thinking about it and . . . and well . . . I just can't . . . '

I dared not speak. If I spoke, it would be like this moment was really happening, so I said nothing. Finally, he turned to me, his eyes heavy with tears.

'It's not that I don't love you,' he said, 'because I do love you, Grace, with all my heart. Please believe me. I'd never loved anyone until I met you.' He laughed a little. 'I never thought I would ever meet anyone I could say those words to so easily. But with you . . . it was different with you.'

I noted the past tense and squeezed my hands together tightly in a ball to stop the pain.

'Was it the party?' I said, my voice sounding low and unfamiliar, as if it belonged to someone else.

JJ shook his head. 'No,' he said. 'The party just confirmed the doubts I'd been having about everything.'

'Doubts?' I said. He had never said anything about doubts before.

'Grace,' he said, finally meeting my gaze. His eyes were watery but they still had that magic sparkle. 'My folks. I can't leave my friends, my family, and my life here. They need me.'

'*I* need you,' I said. I realised it sounded selfish. 'What about our plans? A brighter future away from here. This was our chance, Jay.' The desperation in my voice hung heavy in the drizzle above us. I was trying not to get mad. 'A chance for a new and better life together. Was it something Janice Brady said?' I asked, remembering the snippets of their conversation from the previous night. 'Is she responsible for all this?'

'No, no,' JJ shook his head, placing the package carefully next to him and taking hold of my cold, trembling hands. 'You,' he said gently, as he brushed the wet straggles of hair from my rain- and tear-sodden face. His hands smelled of paint. 'You're clever and amazing and beautiful. You've got a *real* future, Grace. Not like me.'

'But I thought we'd been through all this,' I interrupted, 'all that was before . . . '

'Please Grace, let me finish,' JJ said softly. 'I need you to try and understand. I would never be happy living in the country. You see, when I met you, I was blown away. I couldn't believe someone as classy and intelligent as you would want to be with a drop-out like me. I was taken with the idea that maybe I too could hold my own in a conversation about Shakespeare or poetry, or waffle on about the latest opera as if I knew what I was on about. I really wanted to be that person; someone you would one day be proud of.' He lowered his head. 'Then you went and loved me for who I was anyway and I couldn't believe it. That made me want to do it all the more – get a decent job, build a future, *become someone*.'

'But you *are* someone,' I objected, and then stopped as I realised I had interrupted him again. 'And you are *not* a drop-out.'

'You know what?' JJ said, squinting up through the rain at the sky above him. '*This* is my home. Hamlet Tower, the stinky lift, the cramped, damp flat, the crime and the grime – it's all I've ever known, Grace, and now I realise it's all I ever will know.' He paused for a second. 'I've got roots here, Grace, family and friends. I have my art and my crew. Here, I *am* somebody. I'm JJ off Hamlet estate. I'm Dove the street artist. Down in the Cotswolds, I'll be no one.'

'You'll never be no one,' I said. 'You'll still be JJ wherever you are. *My* JJ. You'll be successful and loved and you'll make new friends and . . .'

I was struck by how familiar my speech sounded. I was repeating all the things Mums had said to me when we had first arrived here.

'But that's just it,' JJ said. 'Success means something different to you. It doesn't make either of us right or wrong. It's just the way it is. I'm not destined for great things, Grace. I'm destined to be here. To live in Hamlet Tower surrounded by what I know. That's all the success I need. I'll never be rich, I'll never be famous and you know, I'm OK with that. Even if I won the lottery I'd probably just end up buying me and Ma a whole floor of the tower!' JJ laughed but it was a horrible, ironic sort of laugh. 'Please don't be angry with me,' he pleaded. 'I tried so hard to want to be different, Grace. I wanted to do it for you, so much. Forgive me.'

I wasn't angry, just desperately sad. I had felt that, by taking JJ away from Hamlet Tower and all the troubles of estate life, I would somehow be saving him. It was never meant to be condescending, yet suddenly that's exactly how it seemed. 'We will remove you from this treacherous hell and make you a real person, a success, a fine upstanding citizen!' I had not believed that anyone could really, truly be happy living life on an estate like Hamlet. But I was wrong.

I rocked back and forth on the bench slightly, my arms wrapped round my chest in a self-preservation hug. I was sure that if I stood up I would fall straight over, knocked sideways by the pain of the dawning truth. I was glad of the rain. It hid my tears.

'Don't hate me, Grace,' JJ said. I looked at his face intently. His dimple had all but disappeared. 'I want you to know that meeting you was the best moment of my life – and now, saying goodbye is the worst.' I opened my mouth to speak. 'Don't say you'll stay here with me. We both know it's not what you want either,' he said, gently touching my lips with his finger. He was right. I couldn't spend the rest of my life at Hamlet Tower, even with JJ.

My phone rang, startling us both. It was Mums. I had

to answer it. I had been gone for longer than fifteen minutes and knew she would be having one of her turns.

'I'll be along soon,' I said before she could speak.

'Where *are* you? We're sitting here like a bunch of buffoons. What is going on?'

'It's OK,' I managed to say. 'Just give me a few more minutes.'

'Is everything all right?' I heard her ask as I snapped my phone shut.

'Mums is waiting,' I said.

'You should go,' JJ said, his hand firmly in mine. Neither of us wanted to let go.

'I suppose I should,' I said. It was hopeless my trying to convince him to come with me. His heart belonged here with his family and all that he knew and loved. Perhaps he would have been unhappy in the Cotswolds anyway, out of place and desperately homesick. I would never have wanted that.

'My life has been better with you in it,' he said.

'Mine too,' I replied huskily, my voice threatening to give up the ghost.

'Really?' JJ said, unconvinced.

'Really,' I said, the tears, unstoppable, sliding down my face.

'Please don't cry,' he said, biting his lip in anguish. 'I hate seeing you cry.'

A sob sneaked out of my throat before I could prevent it.

'Promise me one thing,' he said. 'Promise me that when you're a famous actress you'll think of me sometimes. That you'll never forget me, Grace Foster-Bryce.'

I felt rigid with grief. 'I will never forget you,' I said, trying to contain my sobs. 'How could I?' I half laughed and a great snot bubble shot out of my nose. JJ pulled a tissue from his pocket and handed it to me, just as he had done the first time we met.

'I hope things work out for you,' he said. It sounded so final, like he had already left me and I was staring at his ghost. 'With your mum and dad and everything,' he added. 'I guess he'll be coming home soon and you can get on with your lives together as a family.' I knew he was trying to be kind, to say nice, positive things to make the situation more bearable, but I wished he wouldn't. It hurt so much more to hear him wish me well like a friend.

'Will *you* promise *me* something?' I said, wiping my nose and not caring how snotty I looked any more.

'Anything,' JJ said.

'Promise me you won't end up marrying Janice Brady,' I said.

He started to laugh a little. 'I cross my heart,' he said.

My phone rang again. No prizes for guessing who it was. I didn't answer it.

'I nearly forgot,' JJ said. 'Your Christmas present.' He handed me the big square package he had been carrying, the cheap snowman wrapping paper covering it soggy in the rain.

'But I didn't get you anything!' I was horrified. 'I was planning to buy you something when we got to the Cotswolds . . . '

'Shhhh,' he said. His breath was warm against my cheek. 'It's just a little something I made. I couldn't afford to buy you anything.'

I clutched it to my chest. 'Open it later, on your journey if you like,' he suggested, as if he couldn't bear to watch me unwrap it now.

I nodded. 'I don't want to say goodbye,' I said, knowing that Mums would be having kittens by now and that I had to go.

'Then we won't say it,' he replied.

I felt numb. JJ stood up.

'Kiss me,' he said. 'If you can't say goodbye, just kiss me.'

So I did. I kissed him as if it was my last ever kiss on earth. Perhaps it would be. We stood, together, in the rain, in our pardon, the place where it had all began and now where it would all end, our faces pressed against each other, tears intermingled. We had come full circle.

I didn't look back as I walked away. I couldn't bring myself to. As I walked, I thought of all the things I hadn't said to him: sending my love to his family, that I wanted him to keep on painting and to look out for Jess . . . but I decided he probably knew all those things anyway and that I didn't really need to say them. I thought about maybe saying it all in a letter or a text, an e-mail maybe, but we both knew he would never write. Even if he had been the writing type, I wasn't sure I could bear the inevitability of his correspondence gradually tailing off until one day there would be no more. I wondered how long he had stayed and watched me walk off into the distance. Had he hung on until he could no longer see me or had he just turned and quickly walked away? I guess I would never know.

'Oh Gracie,' Mums said, all anger dissipating in light of the state of my face. 'He's not coming, is he?' I shook my head and ran into her outstretched arms. I cried into my mother's chest for what felt like the longest time, soaking her cashmere cardy and leaving tear stains on her grey T-shirt like I used to when I was a child and had hurt myself.

The journey down to Granny V's cottage would be a long one. I curled myself up in the back seat of Mums's old car next to Cal and clutched the present JJ had given me, unsure whether I had the strength to open it or not. Cal glanced at me at one point, a touching concern on his young face.

'Who needs a surrogate brother anyway,' he said, defiantly, 'when I've got a sister like you?' I held back the tears again as I looked out of the window and watched life in Goldborne Road gradually slip from view, the sound of sirens fading.

# Epilogue

I awoke to the sound of birds singing.

'Grace, Grace! It's been snowing, look!' Cal squealed excitedly as he ran into my nice new – and rather large – bedroom. 'Happy Christmas, sis,' he said, jumping up and down on my bed enthusiastically. 'Get up, get your waterproofs on and let's build a snowman. It'll be wicked, just like old times.'

'Happy Christmas,' I croaked. 'Now do something useful and pass me that dressing gown, will you? It's freezing!'

Downstairs, Mums and Granny V were up and dressed in their finest Christmas attire.

Granny V, sporting a lilac silk crepe two-piece suit with a cream cardigan thrown over her shoulders, looked as dignified as ever. It was obvious who Mums had inherited her sense of style from. Mums was wearing her favourite black trousers and voluminous silk blouse with the pussy bow necktie. Her hair looked glossy and clean and she was smiling. She looked more beautiful than ever.

The cottage smelled of roasting meat and crispy hot fat, and Christmas carols rang out from the old-fashioned stereo. An obscenely large collection of presents lay piled underneath the Christmas tree and a giant glass bowl filled with sweets, satsumas and walnuts in their shells sat on the large dining room table, waiting to be eaten.

'Happy Christmas, my darling.' Mums came towards me and gave me a little squeeze.

'Happy Christmas, Mums,' I replied, hugging her.

I tried to think happy thoughts as I showered and dressed for the day ahead. I had chosen to wear a black silk slip dress with a pale pink shrug over the top, but it was difficult, if not impossible, to shift the hollow ache in my belly. I tried not to think about what JJ might be doing right then, but visions of him taunted me. I pictured his smile, the dimple, and imagined putting my finger on it as I had often done, just to see if it would stop it from dimpling (it didn't). I wondered whether his skin was stubbly, or soft because he had bothered to shave. I could see him and his brothers and sisters all squashed together on that threadbare sofa in their tiny, messy flat as they squabbled and teased each other lovingly. Mary would be in that miniscule kitchenette preparing her frozen turkey and peeling sprouts. She'd probably be singing and swigging gin from a coffee mug. Well, it was Christmas after all.

I laughed softly to myself. 'Happy Christmas, Jay,' I whispered as I blew a kiss into the air, hoping that somehow it might find its way to Hamlet Tower.

'Ta-Dar! Lunch is served,' Mums said triumphantly as she brought the huge steaming bird surrounded by hot crispy potatoes and parsnips to the table on a large platter.

'How about this, darlings? I bet you thought you'd never see the day.'

'I certainly didn't!' Granny V said, giving Cal and me a wink.

Mums began sharpening the carving knife, the sound of metal on metal setting my teeth on edge. 'Well, Mother, these days I'll have you know I am frightfully resourceful. I am chief cook *and* bottlewasher,' Mums said, 'not to mention breadwinner! Here's to a wonderful Christmas and a hap . . . '

We were interrupted by the sound of the doorbell chiming. I went to get it but Granny V beat me to it.

'Blast and I was just about to carve as well,' Mums tutted crossly. 'It had better be something important.'

'. . . or someone,' said a familiar voice as the door opened. 'Shall I carve, Penelope?' he said as he took the knife from her limp hands.

'Edgar,' Mums managed to whisper as he swept her up into his arms. 'Oh my goodness, Edgar darling.'

Dad. My daddy had come home.

The turkey was cold by the time we had all finished hugging and crying but none of us cared a jot. It was still the most magical Christmas lunch any of us had ever tasted.

After we had finished eating, I ushered Cal out of the room. It was only right that Mums and Dad should have a few moments to themselves to say hello properly, like people in love do. Granny V had smiled at me knowingly as I led Cal outside into the crisp coldness. We walked along the shrub-lined path leading away from the cottage and down towards the stream.

'I'm going to build Dad the biggest snowman he's ever seen,' Cal announced as he ran towards a nearby slope. 'Are you going to help me, Grace?'

'I'll come up in a minute,' I called back to him as I wiped the powdery snow from a fallen log by the stream with my gloved hands. I sat down and watched, mesmerised by the icy clear water.

Dad was finally home and, while it was the greatest Christmas present I could've wished for, I couldn't help thinking how I had gained with one hand and lost with another. Instinctively, I wanted to tell JJ the news. All I had to do was pick up my phone and dial his number but I knew I wouldn't. *I couldn't.* The thought of hearing his soft, reassuring voice caused fat tears to form behind my eyes, blurring my vision.

'Oh Jay,' I whispered, allowing the tears to roll down my cheeks, not even bothering to brush them away. I knew he would be so happy for me, for my family. For a moment I imagined that he had come with us to the Cotswolds and that he was there beside me, holding my hand, sharing the moment with me. If things had been different, I wondered whether we would have ever had a real future together, the boy from the estate and the public school girl with a silver spoon in her mouth. Were we really so different at the end of the day? Our backgrounds may have been, but inside we felt the same, of that I felt sure. I cursed myself for not fighting for him harder. He had just been scared, that's all. Scared of change. I could have helped him adjust to his new world just as he'd helped me adjust to mine.

\* \* \*

That night in bed, following a day of love and laughter, a day of new beginnings, the past laid to rest, I unwrapped the present JJ had given me when we had not said goodbye. I carefully opened the neatly sellotaped corners of the flimsy Christmas paper. Inside was a scrapbook filled with cuttings and pictures: our train tickets to Oxshott, a pair of lolly sticks from the ice creams we had eaten in the rain, a photograph of the Piccalilli painting on the railway wall, a flyer for the school performance of *Othello* with my name in bold letters on the front. He had drawn a purple dragosaurus with a speech bubble coming from its mouth that read *JJ and GFB, True Love Always* inside a perfectly symmetrical heart, and he had even taped some grass underneath, with the words, *Memories of a pardon* in his distinctive, artistic scrawl. On the final page was a photograph, the one we had taken of us in Oxshott woods. I had ice cream on my chin and JJ was grinning manically, his dimple more pronounced than ever. Next to the picture, he had written *Every day is ice cream day!* and he'd drawn two little love doves sitting on a perch together. Love doves, together forever. True Love Always.

It was the most beautiful, thoughtful Christmas present I had ever received. No amount of expensive jewellery or designer dresses could ever come close. I closed the book and held it against me as warm tears fell down the sides of my face. I wondered what the future might hold for me now. Now that I faced it alone without Jay. I had heard Mums telling Dad about my performance as Desdemona almost as soon as he had arrived. I even thought I heard them mention the words 'stage school' at one point, though I couldn't be sure it wasn't just wishful thinking.

JJ would be so happy. He had always shown such faith in me and my dreams. A little sob escaped from my throat. I knew in my heart I would never meet anyone else like him, someone who knew what a dragosaurus was, who would keep lolly sticks as romantic mementos or turn my legs to liquid and my heart to a jumping bean every time we kissed. Some people say you only have one great love in your life. I knew that Jay was mine. And now he was gone.

My chest felt tight and heavy as I sucked in breath to prevent more sobs from escaping, but it was no use. Eventually I gave in and let them out, burying my face in my pillow to drown out the sound. I had held out some hope, however flimsy, that maybe JJ would change his mind and come to find me, but in my heart I knew there would be no life for us together in the Cotswolds. JJ would not learn to ride a horse or chop wood for the fire. We would never chase each other through fields, picking blackberries that tasted as sweet as his lips against mine. We would not see winter melt into spring, pick our way through a sea of bluebells in the woods, and lie down together and watch sunrays poke through the trees. I knew that life would go on, but I wished it wouldn't. Time would let me forget about him, my memories gradually floating away like driftwood downstream.

I got up out of bed and moved towards the window, looking out across the perfect white fields that stretched on for miles. I thought about the hundreds of tiny lights that would be burning brightly in Hamlet Tower right about now. I thought about the families, exhausted from the day's excitement, the gangs of kids zooming around on their new BMXs and skateboards that Santa had managed to blag them. And I thought of Mr Dent, the old man at number ninety-three, the soldier who had lived through the war and lost his wife. I guessed he would probably be alone on Christmas Day, still thinking of her, still missing her, even after all these years. I wondered if it would be the same for me and whether, when I am old and alone, I will look back at the picture of JJ and me and think about what might have been.

Although the thought made me sadder than I knew possible, I took solace in something Mr Dent had said.

*True love never really leaves you; it has a home forever – in your heart.*